Skyler Gabriel

Lierre Keith

Fighting Words Press

Published in the United States
Cover design: Lierre Keith
First Edition. First Printing.
Library of Congress Catalog Card Number: 95-60878
ISBN: 0-9632660-2-0
Printed in the United States

This book was made possible
by the generosity of the following women

AMY JESSICA

AN ANONYMOUS WOMAN

ANNIE GARVEY

BETH MCNEIL

GAIL KIELSON

JEAN EMMA FRANCES

JEANNE-MARIE WILD

KERRY TAYLOR

MARY LESBIAN MCCANN

PAM BROWN

SALLY KOPLIN

and especially

ANNEMARIE MONAHAN

SIDNEY SPINSTER

SUSAN GESMER

To Dorian

The Moon and Sun are travelers through eternity.
Even as the years wander on. Whether drifting through
life on a boat or climbing toward old age leading a horse,
each day is a journey and the journey itself is home.

BASHO

Skyler Gabriel

ONE

My name's Skyler Gabriel and I'm the bass player. The band's called Minor Disturbance. Amy thought that up. She's the lead singer.

Everybody wants to know where I got a name like mine. My mom, I shrug. Yeah, so I like being quick, but it's also true. My mother's from Schulyer County, which is in upstate New York. Same pronunciation, different spelling. That's what she wanted to name her first child. Of course she expected it to be a boy, but it wasn't. It was me. She gave me the name anyway. I guess she decided that, realistically, one child was gonna be it. That's noteworthy because my mother's not usually big on reality. She's too big on cheap bourbon.

The Gabriel part was originally Gabrella, but it got anglicized when my great-grandfather immigrated from Italy. I always picture Ellis Island like a kind of giant pasta machine: this big, lumpy mass goes in, and uniform, white lines come out. With a name like Gabriel I was a shoo-in for the angel part in the church Christmas pageant. Catholic church, need I add. Besides the Italian, there's Irish and a little Polish in my family, but the common denominator is definitely Catholic.

Anyway, I met Amy at 911, which is a mixed club in Cambridge. She was singing for this slightly interesting, alternative-type band, Amy being the slight interest. I liked how she sang. She was thin the way boys want women these days, with long legs and thick, dark hair, and I bet the guys in her band wanted her to gyrate around in stupid little outfits, but she didn't. She just sang. She could have gotten brownie points, but went for self-respect. I liked her for it.

I saw her later, leaning up against the wall by herself, looking bored.

"Do you like singing with those guys?" I asked point-blank.

She laughed but still looked bored. "Why?" she asked. I knew what she meant, but I answered another question.

"Because girls kiss better." I don't know what got into me.

She laughed again. Had she already figured me out? A lot of times people can't tell if I'm a boy or a girl. Straight people, anyway. I'm a little too tall, and not the skinny kind like Amy and my hair's short 'cause I like looking like a lesbian.

"I know," she said. The way she smiled, I believed her.

"Good. We're looking for a singer. I play bass, and I've got a guitarist and a drummer. But none of us wanna sing. Not lead, anyway. Wanna come try?"

So she did, and we all liked each other, and thus our band was born.

We even wrote a song together at that first rehearsal. We were all on a roll about whiny white boy music and what the hell did they have to complain about anyway and I started thinking about how those three guys raped me in high school, but I didn't want to get into it. I wondered if Jaye was thinking about her step dad and what Katie had heard on the hotline that week and how much we all still loved our music and our lives. The song came easy.

"What do we call this masterpiece?" Jaye asked from behind her drum kit. Jaye's my roommate. I think she's really cute. Something about her year-round black canvas high-tops, which, in Boston, is no mean feat. No pun intended.

"*I Don't Care,*" Amy suggested. "That's how the refrain should go."

She started singing it perfect. Just the right combination of "fuck you" and "fuck you if you can't take a joke." We couldn't stop laughing.

"So, Amy," said Katie, all soft Southern vowels, and always slow enough to make you wonder what was coming next. "I'll be up front. I think the question is, Are you a lesbian?"

The room got serious though we all tried to keep smiling.

"I don't know," Amy answered with a sigh. "I understand it's important."

There was a second of friendly silence while we all thought about it.

"Oh, I'm gonna be," Amy added, in this resigned, giddy kind of way. "I wanna be with women, but it's not just the sex, it's . . . the everything. You wouldn't believe," her voice dropped to a stage whisper, for added drama, "how different it is singing with the three of you." She sighed and looked at us one by one.

"Can you give me a chance?"

She wasn't begging, either. It was an honest question with that same self-respect. Yeah, she could be a dyke.

Me and Jaye and Katie all looked at each other for confirmation.

"I think we can," I answered. "Right?"

Jaye and Katie both nodded, and then we all jumped for joy.

The night it all started was about a year later. We had a great gig lined up at Freerun Farm, which is lesbian land out near Northampton. They had a small music festival every spring and they asked us to play.

"So, like, Skyler," asked Amy, her fingers drumming a bored, random beat on the steering wheel. "What's going on with you and Judith?" She had on her Who, me? expression, which no one would believe for a second.

I stared out the window, feeling sick and ecstatic and stupid. Face it, Gabriel, it's called love. A red Camaro passed us easily on the right, then cut in front of us with no warning. Amy hit the horn twice but nothing happened. Her car's a really old Chevy—named Evie, of course—with four doors and a huge trunk. It gets about ten feet to the gallon but her grandma gave it to her, so she can't complain. Plus there's room for lots of sound equipment or seven women easy, whichever is more important at the moment. Today it was equipment. Katie and Jaye were in Jaye's car.

Amy gave up on the horn and tilted her head toward the open window.

"Fuck you!" she yelled good-naturedly, then sat back with a contented sigh. I tried not to move, hoping she'd forget about me.

"So?" she asked again after a minute. The thing about Amy is, she may act like life is one long, boring effort, but it's all show. She doesn't miss a thing.

"Nothing," I shrugged, but I didn't look at her.

"Yeah, right," Amy muttered. Just then the speed limit switched from fifty-five to sixty-five and all her concentration shifted to her car.

"Come on, Evie," she coaxed, her face straining as if her whole body, and not just her foot, was doing all the work. "Evie," she moaned. The sound was so pained I almost believed it.

I could have joined in, but it wouldn't have been a game. Not at the moment. I'd fallen in love and I didn't know how and in exactly one hour I'd be with her again. This wasn't like anything else. It was like my heart was some fruit that got peeled, piece by piece, and it could never be undone. Now it lay open and soft, all raw and pink, so easily bruised into pulp. And I had no idea if she could love me back.

Evie had made it to sixty-five. Amy relaxed back and waved vaguely toward the radio.

"Make yourself useful and find me something I can sing."

She was letting me go easy and we both knew it. I clicked on the radio, happy to oblige, happy for the music and the distraction of noise. I made it loud and Amy laughed and whooped and we both started singing. I unrolled my window to feel the warm spring air. In one hour, I'd see Judith.

"You girls sound great," cheered Star from way back. We'd just finished our sound check. The barn was huge, with massive old beams that you could see the ax marks in. The floor was wide, polished boards and I imagined how it would look tonight when we'd send out the beat and women would start moving.

Star's one of the land dykes. She's about fifty and her hair's really short and from what I hear she used to make a point of rinsing her natural menstrual sponge in public bathrooms while singing a song called "Moon Blood Wimmin." Now she talks about menopause as loud as she can whenever she's in line at the bank.

"Well, thank you," said Katie, who never forgets her manners.

"You do sound great," said someone behind me. It was Tanya, another of the land dykes, and beside her was Judith.

"Hi," I stuttered and felt totally stupid. My band began to evaporate. Jaye smirked at me while Amy winked over Judith's shoulder and I began to wish I didn't have friends.

"I've never heard you play before," Judith smiled. A sweet, sweet smile that sank in like soft rain, like something necessary and hoped for. She had on this deep blue shirt that looked so soft. She always wore things like that, teal green or crimson red or chocolate brown, and there was always silver on her wrists and ears.

"Let's go outside," she said, her small hand closing gently around my arm.

She led me out and down a shady brick path. Everything was still damp from yesterday's rain. In the distance I could hear the sound of falling water. I didn't want to talk. It was so quiet now, just the green things making small, small sounds. I wanted to lay Judith down and tend to her here where everything was moist and fragrant and see if she had small sounds, too.

"Those are foxgloves," she said softly, pointing. "That's bleeding heart. That's bloodroot. I should dig one up for you someday. You'll see why they're called that. How's your mom?"

"Out of the hospital. Maybe drinking. I don't know," I said.

She put her arm around my waist and leaned closer. It was a friendly gesture, but it hurt in this funny way. I wanted to tell her more, to tell her everything, I was so sad and no one knew, not even me.

"How've you been?" I asked.

"I'm sick of the print shop. It's so hard to leave the land every morning. But we have to pay the mortgage."

"How's that little one? Hallie?"

"I think she misses Squirrel."

Squirrel is Judith's ex. Of three months, I should add. Judith had told me one night on the phone that they were breaking up, and I really, really tried to be sympathetic, I really, really did, but hope had raised her weary head. Not just raised it, but washed, dried and trimmed it. Squirrel wanted to take some time apart. Gee, I'm so sorry, Judith. Squirrel had moved into town. Oh, I'm so, so sorry, Judith. Meanwhile, hope was shining up her shoes and doing a little dance.

"I think she's lonely, too. She needs other kids."

"Don't Tanya or Nora know other lesbian moms who could live here?"

Judith sighed. "It's not that easy. Most lesbians do artificial insemination, which results in a boy about 80 percent of the time."

"Are you kidding? Why? Is it a plot?"

That made her laugh. "No. It's the difference between X and Y sperm. The X's swim slower but live longer. That'll get you a girl. The dreaded Y's, on the other hand, swim faster but die sooner. Most insemination is done the day of ovulation, which means the Y's win and we lose."

"Well, shit. Why don't more women know that?"

"I don't think they care."

"Poor Hallie," I murmured. I like kids in the abstract. It's in the concrete that I run into trouble. "Ooh, what are those?"

"Skyler, you're a land dyke at heart. Those are wild lupines. They're native to this continent and they're good for the soil."

"The first time I came here you were planting irises. I remember you were so excited. They blooming yet?"

"Ah, my irises. Some of them," she nodded. "Want to see?"

She led me down another path and up some stone

steps and she still had her arm lightly around my waist. At the top was a bank of purple flowers and all I could do was stare. Okay, I'm a city kid. I swear I didn't know that irises looked like that. We both stood very still, the soft, crinkley folds of the irises wide open before us.

"Have a seat," Judith said eventually, pointing to a weathered wooden bench.

"Okay, Skyler," she stopped and sighed. Then she laughed. "So I've got a thing for you. But it'll never work so we're just going to have to get over it."

It was all I needed and it was everything. Hope began singing at the top of her lungs.

"Why?" I asked, trying not to look at her mouth.

"Because I'm just getting out of a long-term relationship."

"Bad break-up?" I murmured sympathetically.

"Actually, it was a long time coming."

"So what's the problem?"

"You're too clever for your own good. I'm also Jewish and it's important to me."

"I'll convert."

She threw back her head and laughed. I could see tiny lines on her throat.

"I'm a separatist," she argued.

"Well, I'm not, but I'm sympathetic." Her eyes were smiling. I knew I was winning. "I never met a man I liked."

"It's more than that. You're twenty-four years old. I'm thirty-two."

"I've been out since I was fourteen. That's ten years. How about you?"

"It's a different milieu."

"No," I said, sitting up straighter. "I know what you mean, but I'm not afraid to say words like lesbian or feminist or to put them together. And neither are my friends."

"You're just a baby," she said.

I don't kiss like one, I wanted to say, but I didn't. I showed her instead.

The band sounded great that night. The place was

packed and there was something wild happening, the warm air on our bare arms, the sweet smell of earth and women's skin. Amy took it to the edge and I was right behind her the whole way while women danced and shouted and the lights went down lower. We didn't even break between songs, we just kept it coming, an old Pretenders' tune, Amy's punked-out version of Suzanne Vega's *Undertow*, a U2 song, then one of mine and I caught a glimpse of Judith grinning at me and the music kept on and on. I was in an altered state when we wound up with *Because the Night*, I sing back-up on that one but it wasn't me singing, it was some angels, those lesbian angels that ache in your heart for one more try, and Judith stood in the shadows, just watching.

Even when the lights came on, the spell didn't quite break. We'd been invited to spend the night, but we couldn't. Amy had to waitress Sunday brunch, so we loaded up the equipment and tried to feel the ground again. There were candles lit along the path and the night was a deep quiet, waiting and full, and the sky had so many stars it made me thirsty.

"Here you go," said Star, handing us the take for the dance, as per our agreement.

"How much?" Jaye asked.

"I didn't count," Tanya said. "Over two hundred."

I was only vaguely paying attention. Judith was watching me, smiling, and I was trying to kiss her with my eyes.

"Thanks again," said Tanya. Her partner, Nora, held their sleeping child in her arms.

"You can come back any time. You were fantastic!" added Star.

Judith stepped up to me. "I'll call you," she said quietly so no one else could hear. But then she kissed me, and everyone saw.

I thought about irises the whole way home.

Actually it was $300. Divided by four was $75 each and I owed Amy $50, so I took it out of my share.

"One hundred and twenty five dollars," Amy said, almost drunk on it. For people like us it's a fortune. "We better stop at the bank machine so I can deposit it."

There's a little ATM kiosk near my apartment, in the parking lot of a supermarket complex. Amy pulled up and left the engine running.

"I'll do it," I offered. "You man the equipment." Though truth be told, it's the car I'm afraid for. Not that someone will steal it, but that it'll stall and never start again.

"Woman the equipment," Amy corrected.

"Yeah, you're right. What's your secret number?"

"Eight, four, two, zero. Put it in my checking account. I don't have a deposit envelope, you'll have to fill one out. What *is* the right word, anyway?"

"No trouble. Back in a flash."

I got out of the car. The night was still so warm.

"Staff. You staff the phones or the table or whatever," I said through the window.

"Okay, I'll staff the equipment, you staff the ATM."

The kiosk has three machines. It's kind of an "L" shape and I don't like it late at night because you can't see who's around the bend. At the first machine there was a short bald guy with a bow tie and a resigned curve to his spine. In other words, unthreatening. I walked around the "L" to the other machines. Nobody. Good.

I get sick of that feeling of fear. It starts in your stomach and you can't stop it. The best I can do is pretend. Someday when I have money, I'm gonna take model mugging. It should be free for all women, along with child care, tampons and taxis. If I ruled the world.

I stuck the card in the slot. What the hell did Amy say her number was. I felt like a ten-year-old playing secret spy games. Eight, two, four, zero, I punched in. Something like that.

Sorry, your password is incorrect. Please try again.

I could hear the smooth tone of voice, even though it wasn't spoken. Yet. The wonders we have to look forward to in the twenty-first century.

Okay, maybe eight, two, zero, four. Beep, beep,

beep, beep went the happy little machine in the most annoying way.

Sorry, your password . . . flashed up on the screen again. The bald guy was gone so I cursed out loud. I wondered if I should cancel the whole thing and get the card back. I've heard you only get three tries before the machine confiscates your card and it didn't seem fair to try it out at Amy's expense. Then again, I was feeling kind of reckless, what with spring and Judith and the performance and all. Okay. Eight, four, two, zero.

It worked. The rest was easy. Deposit. Beep. Checking Account. Beep. $125. Beep. The metal door slid open with a click. I grabbed a deposit envelope and started filling it out.

I heard someone else enter the kiosk. It's like a technological pagoda where we all come to worship. My unseen cell mate was apparently already attuned. The beep-beep-beeps went quickly.

"Come on," she whispered under her breath. "Come on."

"Damn!" she swore loudly. "I've exceeded my limit? I've got the money in there, for God's sake!"

Oh, the traumas of modern living. She must not have realized she had company.

I'd finished filling out the deposit envelope and was licking it shut when somebody else came in. I heard the woman gasp.

"Get away from me," she said, her voice cold and serious. I froze mid-lick.

"Where's your daughter?" a man asked, slow and taunting.

"None of your goddamned business," she spat. She was moving toward the door. I could see her now in the reflection of the windows. It was so dark out the glass made perfect mirrors.

He put an arm out to block her way. If he had touched her I was ready to spring, but he didn't. She stopped instead.

"What do you want?"

"You know what I want."

"Get out of my way," she said, raising her chin defiantly. She had brown hair pulled back in a fraying braid and a small face with big eyes.

He laughed and stepped into my line of reflected vision. He was tall and blond and looked basically like he owned the world. Men like that give me the creeps, even when they're not threatening women and their girl children.

"And if you don't leave me alone, Doctor, I'll get a restraining order."

"Doctor? Surely we're past formalities."

She stared at him for a second before replying. "That probably was intimacy for you."

"Does Chloe miss her father?"

She almost flinched, but didn't. Her mouth tightened.

"You realize that if the police find, say, another bag of cocaine in your car, your child might as well be an orphan, for all the time you'll get to spend with her."

"That was you, wasn't it?"

"Diane, Diane," he said with a smile. "And what are you doing at the bank at twelve-thirty on a Saturday night? A sudden need for cash?"

"Get out of my way," she repeated coolly. She wasn't scared, or if she was, she didn't show it. She called his bluff and started walking. At the last second, he pulled his arm away. She pushed open the door.

"Leave me alone," she said over her shoulder.

He laughed and watched her through the glass. Then he left, too.

I took a breath and realized it had been a few minutes since my last one. His cologne, something expensive and almost subtle, hung in the air. I put the deposit envelope in its slot and watched the machine swallow it. It spit the card out at me after a few compulsory clicks and whirs. I grabbed it and tried not to run.

The night air woke me up to the sweat on my skin. I looked around but the only car in sight was Amy's.

"What took you so long?" she grumbled as I handed her the card. "Where's my receipt?"

"Fuck, Amy. I forgot it. It'll be all right."

"It was cash, Skyler."

"Let's just get the hell out of here, okay?"

"Hey, you all right?" she said, pulling into the street.

"Yeah, it's just that . . ." I didn't know what to tell her. "This man was harassing this woman at the ATM. It was weird. I didn't know what to do, but she handled it. Sorry about the receipt."

"Don't worry about it, " she said, nodding. She floored the accelerator and cranked up the volume.

The air rushed in as the streets rushed by, smelling of rain and earth and promising us summer. We sang at the top of our lungs and it was okay just to be alive.

And I didn't even know what was coming.

TWO

Me and Jaye live in J. P. That's Jamaica Plain, a section of Boston that didn't get totally devastated, i.e., renovated, during the gentrification of the Eighties. Actually, a lot of lesbians, students, artists, and other "undesirables" kind of trickled into J. P. as we got squeezed out of other places. It's a little run down but basically a great place. There's a lot of really cool old houses and winding one-way streets, which are probably a pain for driving, but since I don't have a car, it's not a problem.

I have a bike. Not a motorcycle. A real bike. It's a black mountain bike with twenty-one speeds and index shifting. I love this bike. I would do anything for this bike. She's my trusty Steed. I keep my wrenches and tools in a kit by the door, in case of emergencies, and I always have a rag in my back pocket so I can wipe her off if it rains. Steed lives in luxury on our little sun porch. She's kind of heavy to carry up and down two flights, but love sometimes requires sacrifices, and anyway, I'm pretty strong.

So just before noon I carried Steed down to the street and set off for brunch. Amy can serve me up for free if I get there after the morning rush. My food stamps hadn't arrived yet and pickin's were getting pretty slim. I'd been eating potatoes for three days, through that low-blood sugar, protein-deprivation induced kind of low-level nausea, and it was having an aversion therapy affect. I didn't want to look at them. The only other option was cheap elbow macaroni, but I didn't have any butter, let alone sauce. But it was gonna be all right. They'd fed us great last night and Amy would fortify me for shopping. I still had $25 in my pocket from the performance, for when the co-op opened at noon.

The restaurant's in Brookline Village, which is a nice bike ride from J. P. It's a macrobiotic restaurant.

"A what?" I'd asked when Amy told me where she worked.

"Macrobiotic," she repeated slowly, blowing the bangs out of her eyes in her bored Amy way.

"Is that like for super people?"

She blinked and dropped her chin an inch. "What are you talking about?"

"The Biotic Man," I urged.

"That's *bionic*, Skyler."

"Biotic, bionic, who cares? It was re-runs and I was young," I defended. I'd secretly wanted to be the Biotic—Bionic—Man when I was a kid. The re-runs were on every day from four to five, right before my mother got home and started drinking. He always had some exhausting physical trial, like he had to run and run and run, or swim through ice, or lift thirty tons of train off a baby, and it hurt him but he always did it, because he was the only one that could. Then he'd be in the hospital and they'd have to repair him but it was okay. I would imagine the pain, the desperation, that final, physical act that only I could do, until bruised and bloodied I succeeded. Then waking in the cool, white sheets, with my wounds bathed and wrapped, and everyone loved me for what I had suffered. The pain was noble, the sacrifice beloved, the world was righted and evil subdued. Yes, I grew up Catholic. How did you guess?

The sun was up and so was the city, in a lazy Sunday kind of way. The air was too cool for just my t-shirt, but I didn't mind. Actually, I hate extraneous clothes. "Overdressed" to me means too hot. It's like some people don't know what to do with their hands, and so they feel awkward if they're not smoking or something, but for me it's clothes. What do you do with a jacket that you're not wearing? How do you hold it? It's too bulky to tie around your waist and it invariably falls off the back of your chair in the restaurant and gets stepped on and then you feel stupider because it has shoe tread in brown all over it. Why does this torture me? Do other people have these problems?

But the sun was shining and the trees were one notch greener and the mud was almost gone. We have five seasons in Boston, mud being the fifth. It starts sometime in March and it is not a pretty sight. Piles of slush, gone gray-brown from the car exhaust, hanging out on every street corner like listless lumps of Christmas Past. And everywhere the ground shows through it's matted with last years brown, soggy grass, packed down with footprints.

But somehow the green returns, first with little flowers, and then the buds on the trees ripening like fruit, and you can hear the birds singing again. And on days like today, winter fades like a bad dream.

I locked Steed to a No Parking sign and sauntered around the corner into the restaurant. The Five Grains, it's called.

"What are they?" I'd asked Amy, more than once, but all she was sure of was brown rice.

She saw me and waved and gave me a nice table by the window.

"The usual?" she asked. In a parallel universe, Amy chewed gum, nuked her hair blond, and worked in a diner in Montana. I guess I'd be her biker boyfriend, with a Harley tattoo and slim-fitting jeans.

"Whatever's easy," I nodded. "You ever been to Montana?"

She just blinked, knowing better than to ask.

The restaurant was pretty quiet. It's the kind of place that sometimes make me restless. Not because it's boring or anything, but because it's so nice. The exposed brick, the huge, old windows, the warm brown floor and wooden chairs. And then the people. Their clothes were soft and svelte and cotton, a lot of them handmade, not because they were poor but because they could afford it. The woman across from me had shoulder length hair smooth as water, her rose sweater closed with silver buttons, no stains, nothing frayed, her mouth an unhurried, softly colored smile. Was there a lesbian version somewhere, a womanist world of abundance and hand-dyed cloth? With no one on top and no one on the bottom, no pyramid with the lucky few at the pinnacle well-educated in extracting without noticing the human price?

I thought of Judith and her lesbian land. Was there a city version for dykes like me?

Sure, it's called J. P., I wanted to laugh. The women's bookstore, the lesbian-owned bakery, the natural food co-op . . . Still, you needed money. Always, money.

I spotted an abandoned newspaper and grabbed it. It was the late edition. The front few sections were gone, but I didn't care. It was the Help Wanteds I needed. My unemployment was only good for another six weeks, and then what.

But I never got to the employment section. Staring up at me from a photo was the woman from the ATM machine. "Diane Frasier," read the caption. "Playwright Found Dead In Brookline Home; Suicide Suspected," was the headline.

"Uh uh, no way," I muttered out loud. The woman in the sweater glanced up at me. I pretended not to notice.

There was no way that woman—Diane—had killed herself. She'd been so . . . alive.

Yeah, real bright, Gabriel. Isn't everyone before they're dead?

All right, stubborn then. And defiant. And she had to protect her daughter from the Bad Man.

Right about then Amy plunked down my organic whole-grain pancakes with transitionally grown blueberries and 100 percent pure, locally-harvested maple syrup. She also handed me a bag filled with something warm and yummysmelling.

"For later," she whispered. She was gone before I could tell her about Diane.

I read and reread the article while I ate. It was definitely her. No question there. Diane Frasier. Apparently she was a semi-famous playwright. Her work had been produced off-Broadway and in Europe and had at times been controversial because of her political stands. In *Back Alley Memoirs* she had collected women's stories of their illegal abortions and turned them into a one-woman show. It sounded great. I'd never heard of it, but theater isn't really my thing.

The police said the probable cause of death was an overdose of prescription drugs. Her daughter, Chloe Frasier, age four, had discovered the body around 2 AM Geez, poor kid. Waking from one nightmare into a worse one.

And where was Chloe now? The paper didn't say.

Though it mentioned that Diane's husband, Jonathan, had died last year. That's when I got really nervous. Surely there must be family. Surely the evil doctor couldn't have gotten his hands on her. Right?

It's not any of my business, I recited to myself, chewing determinedly. Sure. And that's exactly what everyone says and half the reason why the world's such a fucking mess. It's not my business when the woman next door is screaming for help. It's not my business as the cattle cars roll by, filled with human cargo.

Okay, so it's my business, I admitted, stabbing a juicy blueberry. I know the Bad Man was threatening her with something, but I don't know who or how or why. I don't have anything to go the police with. Officer, this woman was murdered. How do I know? I just feel in my heart, very very strongly, I feel a man I can't tell you anything about killed her.

There's nothing I can do.

Sure, and that's the other reason the world's a you-know-what. Everyone lets themselves feel so powerless. Can't fight City Hall. Might as well lie back and enjoy it. Well, fuck that. Collaboration's never been my style.

There was an address in the paper. I could start there.

And do what?

I didn't know, as I sighed and stacked the dishes in a neat pile. But what I did know was that there was a four-year-old girl who needed protection and no one knew that except me.

I ripped the article out of the paper and headed out the door.

THREE

It was a nice house, but Brookline's like that. I'd had to ask directions at a gas station but the street had been easy to find. I parked Steed around the corner and approached on foot. The street was lined with well-kept Victorians and the Frasiers' was no exception. Peach with black trim and two stained glass windows. There was a birdbath in the front yard, and round back, I could see a swing hanging from a tree limb. It was motionless in the still air, but I wanted to imagine the little girl shrieking with laughter while her mother pushed her higher.

More, she'd yell, her hands sticky from some childhood treat, her little overalls patched at the knees where she'd fallen once too often.

If I push you too high, you'll start growing feathers, her mother replies. That's what happens to kids sometimes.

Then what? Chloe demands, still laughing.

Then the only way to get the feathers off children is for their parents to throw them in the bathtub and keep them there for a few days.

No! she laughs and laughs, as the swing goes higher, still higher.

But nothing moved. The swing, the curtains in the windows, the front door. Inside I bet a kitchen clock was ticking, but that was all. Normally there would have been the television, the constant motion of a four-year-old, the sound of eggs frying, the smell of orange juice, but suddenly nothing. Did the house feel like it had had a miscarriage?

It was just after one o'clock. Everybody had had their bagels, and now they were reading the paper. There was nobody around. I acted like I belonged there, in case anyone was watching, and strolled confidently down the driveway. There was a porch on the back of the house. I climbed the stairs and peeked in through the window. Everything was white: white stove, white tile floor, white cabinets. The kind of kitchen you only see in magazine ads.

There was a screen between me and the window and I had to get through it to see if the window was unlocked. I'd done this enough as a kid to know it wasn't hard. Not at strangers' houses or anything (*I Was A Teenage Burglar*), just at my own. My mom was working and I'd lose my key or lock myself out. It felt too familiar for me to be nervous. Besides, I hadn't done anything yet.

I couldn't pop the screen out of its track. It was too nice and new for that. Oh well. Diane and Chloe would have to forgive me. I used my keys and poked a nice finger-sized hole in each bottom corner. I reached in and got the screen up easy.

Then that moment of truth. It was spring in a good neighborhood and the window was above the sink. The odds were in my favor. I pushed gently upward on the window. It opened effortlessly. I was in.

The first scary moment was sitting on the windowsill looking down into the sink. Once I swung my legs up and over, I would be completing the "entering" part of "breaking and entering." It was now or never. I could go home instead, listen to Jaye's new CD player, practice my bass, mope around by the phone in case Judith called . . .

But I had to. Diane had appointed me guardian and she hadn't even known it. My feet touched the sink. I was really in.

For a single mom, the house was immaculate. It was another one of those magic moments when you realize what a difference money makes. There wasn't a crumb in sight.

So what was in sight? What was I looking for? I hopped to the floor. Just absorb, I told myself. God is in the details, didn't somebody say? If God wanted me to help Chloe, She'd better give me some pretty clear details.

I opened the refrigerator. Yogurt, 2 percent milk, some poppy seed bakery bread, sliced turkey, apple juice, lettuce, pretty standard stuff. The freezer had peas, Ben & Jerry's, and Stouffer's frozen lasagna. Gee, I was learning a lot. The Frasiers weren't vegetarians.

The bottom floor was laid out in squares. There were four rooms of basically equal size, each one opening into the two that bordered it, with a staircase in the middle. From the kitchen, one doorway led into a dining room, the other into a laundry and storage area. I went for the dining room.

It had beautiful furniture, kind of Shaker-esque chairs and tables, in one of those hardwood deals that glows, maple or cherry or something. There were flowers on the sideboard with a card propped against them.

"Happy Birthday! Love, Ruth and Gideon," it read. I made a mental note of the names.

Next was a small hallway, with the front door to my left and the stairs directly opposite. Straight ahead was the living room. It was so quiet. I realized I was tiptoeing and not really breathing.

"There's no one here," I said out loud, partly to bolster my own courage. It didn't work. I just felt stupid on top of scared.

The living room had those cushy couch units arranged in an L around a glass-topped table. *The Book of Gardens* and *Ireland: Land of Magic* were the titles on the glossy book covers. On the wall hung a contemporary quilt in strips of satiny blues and purples. There was a shelf of CD's and cassettes, some jazz but mostly classical. On the floor by the couch was a brown leather purse.

I snatched it up and took a look inside. Diane Frasier, said the first thing I pulled out, a bound address book. Bingo. This could be a gold mine.

Movement caught my eye. I ducked back into the hall, heart pounding. Through the window, I saw an elderly couple stroll by. Either they hadn't seen me or they didn't know to care. I waited until they had passed before I moved again. I was starting to sweat.

Figuring that upstairs would be more personal, I skipped the back room and headed up, slinging the purse over my shoulder. Finders, keepers. This was another scary moment, pushing the ambiguous boundary of my crime. Wandering around downstairs, well, that was one thing. But going up into their bedrooms? There'd really be no turning back. I wiped my palms on my jeans.

The second floor was basically the same layout,

only it looked considerably more lived in. Guess the cleaning lady didn't do bedrooms. The first room was obviously Chloe's. A child-size table and chairs, a large stuffed elephant, crayons and paper, lots of books, a wooden bureau hand-stenciled with leaves. It was a cute room and everything looked okay, but then I didn't know what wouldn't.

I opened the top dresser drawer and poked around. There was a stack of little white undershirts, a pile of underpants, and a jumble of colored socks. I shut the drawer and peeked into the closet. There were child-size dresses on child-size hangers, with Barney sneakers and a pair of snow boots on the floor.

All right, on to the next room. It was Diane's and it was a mess. The bureau drawers were half open and clothes were hanging out like they were escaping. Nice clothes, need I add. The bed was unmade, and there were books and shoes in scattered clumps along the deep burgundy carpet. I spotted a large nylon travel bag by the open closet. The bag was half full. Inside there were underclothes, jeans, a cable knit sweater, and assorted toiletries. The question was: was she leaving or returning? Judging from the state of her room, this bag could have been here for weeks. Then again, packing in a hurry could reduce anybody's tidy life to this kind of federal disaster area.

There was a doorway that led into a study, and a door beside it to her bathroom. I opted for the bathroom. It had blue and purple tile and a claw foot tub. Her bathrobe lay draped across a white wicker hamper. There was a matching trash can which held a J. Crew catalog, a couple of tampon applicators and an empty box of hair dye. I opened the mirrored medicine chest. It looked pretty standard: baby aspirin, allergy medicine, hydrogen peroxide. On the bottom shelf, right in front sat two duplicate pill bottles. They caught my eye because they were exactly the same. I picked them up to read the labels but that was when I heard the voices.

Yes, the unmistakable sound of human beings communicating. There were people downstairs. Fuck.

Still holding the pills, I was out of the bathroom in two steps, and suddenly thankful for the plush carpet. It muffled my beeline through the bedroom to the hall, and then my quick retreat backward. Somebody had started up the stairs. Shit, fuck, what was I gonna do? The closet.

"Be thorough, but let's not stay too long," a man's voice directed.

I reached the open closet and dove for the back. She had a lot of clothes and I was making too much noise. I grabbed for the knob and pulled the door but it wouldn't shut all the way. There were a few too many Ann Taylor suits. Damn it. The footsteps were coming down the hall. I gave up fighting the doorknob and held my breath. Through the crack in the door I could see first one and then another boy enter the bedroom. They were both white, around twenty, wearing very neat-looking jeans and t-shirts. One was tall, probably six feet, with blond hair. The other guy was short and stocky with a brown crew cut, which would have looked cute on your average lesbian, but boys with crew cuts aren't usually very nice.

"It's kind of weird," Blondie said in an expressionless voice. His speech was slow and the vowels had a midwestern flatness.

Fuzzy Wuzzy made a sort of grunt in response. The intelligence of men never ceases to amaze me.

"Let's start in here," Blondie said.

They came right toward the closet. For one wild second I thought about throwing the door open, yelling at the top of my lungs, and running while I still had the element of surprise on my side. I had my scream in place, lungs full, throat ready, body tensed for flight, when I realized they had passed me. Blondie meant the study, not the closet. I let out my breath.

I could hear drawers opening and papers rustling. I swallowed hard and tried to focus on seconds, details, the minutiae of the experience. There was a hanger jabbing me in the back of the neck. Diane's clothes smelled slightly sweet, something floral and feminine. I still had her purse hanging off my elbow, and I was clutching the two pill bottles. The seconds ticked by.

All time runs parallel, I thought to myself. New Age platitudes to the rescue. This, too, shall pass.

"What's it look like?" a different voice. Must be Fuzzy Wuzzy. "I mean, will it say 'will' right on it?"

So they were looking for her will?

"I guess. It's probably obvious," came the long, slow reply.

"Well, it's not on the desk."

"The file cabinet—," this guy must put himself to sleep talking, "— isn't in alphabetical order." Oh, we know our ABC's. "You check the bedroom."

Oh shit. My heart started gearing up for the Indy 500. Holy Mary, Mother of God, just get me out of this alive, I started praying. Funny how it comes back, like people whose accents come out when they're upset.

But Fuzz Head passed up the closet in favor of the bureau. I wanted to smell Diane's perfume again, there was something so soothing about it, like how a mother should smell, but my sweat was too strong with the smell of fear. I watched him through the crack in the door as he rifled through the clothes. He picked up a bra and held it up by the straps. He's going to go home and masturbate to the memory of the dead woman's bra, I thought, teeth clenched. I hate men.

"Can you help tomorrow?" asked Slow Poke.

"I've got Rosenberg in the morning. Makes me sick, fucking faggot Jew at 8 AM."

I heard myself gasp. He meant it, too, with that superiority bigotry gives people, his mouth drawn up ugly and tight.

"After that I'm free."

I was afraid he'd heard me, but he kept rifling through her drawers. He had two more to go. After that, the closet was the only other place to look.

You are scum, I chanted in my head. It was the best I could do, since I was in no position to confront him.

"Hey, did you see her purse was missing?" he added. "The cops must have taken it."

Blondie's laugh was as long and dry as a South Dakota summer.

Fuzz Boy shut the last drawer. My moment of reckoning was here. Back to plan A: throw open the door, scream bloody murder, and run for your life. That's if your knees don't give way first. Those few seconds went on forever, he was turning toward me, one step, two, I took a deep breath, he was reaching for the doorknob, the door was opening—

"Hey, I think I found it!"

"Really?" His hand fell away. I heard his footsteps into the other room. The crack in the door was a good six inches wider, but he hadn't seen me. I could feel the sweat backing up in my eyebrows. I wanted to shut the door so bad. Please, God, get me out of this. Please, please, I'll do anything. Was I praying to a Him or a Her? Did I care? It was hard to believe my masculine friends couldn't hear my heart, which was working like a jack hammer in my chest.

"The file says 'will' but I don't think any of this is a will," said Mr. Minnesota. There was a moment of silence. I could almost hear the gears creaking oh so slowly in their little brains.

"Let's go show the doctor."

Doctor? The same doctor from the ATM? The Bad Man?

And out they marched in descending order, passing right by me again. I heard them in the hall, then down the stairs.

This was my chance. I dropped the pills into the bag and headed straight for the door. I could hear voices downstairs, but couldn't make out what they were saying. I left behind the muffled safety of the carpet for the creaking hardwood hallway, then paused at the top of the stairs. Should I hide somewhere else instead? In Chloe's room or something? Down below I could see the front door was wide open.

As I stood there, someone walked across the hallway, another young guy, in blue jeans and a striped oxford. From the living room, right below me, to the dining room. I didn't even pray, my emotions too much movement. I just stood absolutely still and counted his steps. One, two, three, four. He didn't look to the side and he didn't see me. Then he was gone. I heard him walk through the dining room.

That was it. I wanted out.

It was the longest flight of stairs I ever descended. Also the loudest. I clutched Diane's purse to my side like a life preserver the whole way down, and hoped to heaven they were all too far back to see me. I could hear male voices, but couldn't make out the words. Once down, I sprinted across the hallway, my tiptoed feet with a will of their own. The screen door opened easily and I only waited long enough to make sure it wasn't going to slam behind me.

Then I ran.

FOUR

I had planned on visiting my mother after brunch since she lives in Brighton, which is next door neighbors with Brookline. It was two o'clock when I arrived, and the warm day was coaxing out more and more casual strollers. Steed and I had toured our way through Brookline for awhile to calm me down and summon up a mother state of mind. I was as ready as I was gonna be.

The door to her second floor apartment didn't have a doorbell or a knocker, but an old handwritten sign instructed, "Knock loud or I can't hear you!" There was also a brightly colored poster that read, "It Took Me 40 Years To Look This Good!" Oh, Ma. Somebody'd probably given it to her as a get well present.

The door opened and there she was. My little mother. Sometimes you don't remember how much you love someone until you see them again. She looked better, the sick yellow color almost gone from her skin. Her blue eyes looked lively and she was wearing a dressing gown covered with tropical fruit.

"Skyler," she said and hugged me but didn't smile. Push and pull, yes and no, that was my mother.

"Come in, why are you standing in the hall? Where's your coat?"

"It's warm out, Ma. I didn't need one."

"You're gonna get sick. And you can't get sick 'cause you don't got insurance."

"No, don't worry. When you're on unemployment you get great benefits. I have a MassHealth card. I've probably got better coverage than you."

She snorted. "So that's what I'm supposed to tell my family? My daughter's on welfare but she's got great health benefits."

"Ma, it's not welfare, it's unemployment. And I don't care what you tell your family."

"Why don't you go back to school?"

"Can we sit down somewhere?"

"Sure," she smiled and then laughed. "Let's go into my room. I can lie down."

I was happy with that. There was a living room, but the furniture all had those plastic slipcovers so it made you sweat to sit on anything. I followed her down the hall.

She got in bed and leaned back against a pile of pillows. The television sat on her old bureau, blasting away some cable reruns. On the wall above was a 1950's portrait of the Virgin Mary. My mother picked up a burning cigarette and took a long drag.

"So how've you been?" I asked, settling myself on the bed.

"I'm gonna go back to work this week. I'm okay."

"Yeah? What's the doctor say?"

"What do doctors know? He says if I'm feeling up to it."

Doctors know when people are sick, I wanted to say. And they know why. Like getting drunk every night can severely increase your susceptibility to hepatitis.

"If you're gonna lecture, don't bother. That's what I got a doctor for." Her eyes drifted over my shoulder to the television. I watched her face, lined from too much worry and too many cigarettes, and never enough money in a huge and strange city.

Her eyes refocused on me. "So Marilyn was here yesterday for lunch. You wanna hear this? Her daughter," she leaned toward me, "her daughter Theresa got a bonus two weeks ago, 'cause she works for an accountant and tax season was over? So Theresa gets this bonus and she drives down to Atlantic City—she took $200 and made $3,000 playing the cards." She stopped mid-story to take another drag.

"So then she has to split it with her nigger boyfriend—"

"Ma!" I sat bolt upright. What was this, National Bigotry Day? "Why do you have to say shit like that?"

"Don't use that kind of language with me, Skyler Marie," she replied fiercely.

Skyler Marie. We were in for a doosie.

"I'd rather call shit 'shit' then call people 'shit'."

"I don't think all black—"

"No. Forget it, Ma. You can't use that word."

"You can't come into my house and tell me what to do."

We both had our chins stuck out in exactly the same way.

"Oh yes I can. When you act like a stupid racist bigot. You know a hundred years ago Catholics were considered an inferior race, Italians and Irish and Polish. People had the same attitude toward us, Ma, me and you, that you have about black people. There were signs on doors that said, "No Catholics." And there was white slavery, too, you know. People like us were slaves. Not just servants, but slaves."

"You're only half Catholic," she dismissed me.

"Ma," I said in three, impatient syllables. "That's not the point."

"You look so much like your father sometimes. Of course, if you'd dress like a girl, it might not be so noticeable."

I glared at her.

"So don't you want to hear the end of the story?"

"Yeah, okay," I gave in. It never ended with my mother and I was too tired to keep pushing right now. I sighed and felt like shit. "Can I turn the tv off?"

"Why are you always trying to tell me what to do?"

"I'm not telling you what to do. I'm asking you for permission to turn off the television so I can hear what you're saying."

"Fine. Turn it off."

I reached behind me but she beat me to it with a remote control, then laughed at her own gag.

"Where'd you get one of those?"

"Edna next door got it for me, 'cause I was sick."

"See? Edna's not white."

"Who cares? Edna's okay. Anyway," she began emphatically, "so here's Theresa in Atlantic City with $1500, so she keeps playing only now she starts losing. When she's down to $700, she quits. Figures she's still ahead. And her and the boyfriend leave the casino and go back to the car only the car's gone. Stolen. So they have to go to the police station and file a report and then they had to take the bus home." She paused here to stamp out her cigarette butt.

"Well, a week later, she gets this call from a garage down there and guess what? The car wasn't stolen. It was parked illegally, and the garage had towed it. It had been sitting in their lot for a week. So to get her car back she had to pay a fee for each day it was there, and for the towing, and a fine to the police. She had to pay $800 to get her car back. $800. So she was out a hundred bucks."

"Don't it figure," I shook my head.

"I hope she doesn't marry that guy."

"Ma," I warned.

"Well, at least she'll be getting married," she said pointedly, but she was grinning.

"Hey, if marriage is so great why didn't you do it?"

"'Cause your father was a lousy bastard." The irony of the insult was lost on her.

"Well, then it was no big loss, was it?"

For a second, she didn't know whether to be amused or angry, but she laughed and I was glad. I tried to imagine my mother, seventeen years old and pregnant in that tiny town. Abortion was illegal and anyway she was Catholic. And Christopher, that was his name, wouldn't marry her. Tall like me, with light brown hair and poet's eyes. I found a picture of the two of them sitting on the hood of his car. He wanted to go to college, far away, so he left her with the baby they'd made growing bigger every day. She told her mother who told her father, who threw her out of the house. I don't know why she picked Boston, she almost never talks about it, but that's where she landed and where I was born.

"I'm gonna get some juice. You want some? I got orange and I got some kind of grape-berry stuff. My doctor said to drink plenty of fluids," she added, like she was proving a point.

"No, I just ate."

I lay down while she puttered in the kitchen. She'd moved into this apartment when I'd left for school. It's only one bedroom so it's more affordable, but there weren't very many windows, so you couldn't see trees or sky. The paint, once crisp white, was turning a dreary beige from time and smoke. I wished she'd let me repaint for her.

My mother came back in and plumped up her pillows once before settling down in bed.

"Why'd you choose Boston," I asked gently, "when you left home?"

"Why?" She lit up a cigarette while she considered. "I had a cousin who'd moved here. She was a little older than me. Regina. I just turned up on her doorstep. But family's family. She helped me a lot when you were born. She thought you were the cutest thing . . ."

"Where is she?" I was sitting up now. "How come I never heard about her?"

"She's dead," Ma said, tapping the ashes off her cigarette with more force than it could ever need. "She married a Navy man when you were almost a year. Took her all over the place. I told her she wouldn't be happy, and I was right. He beat her, too. Son-of-a-bitch. I learned one thing from my mother. You don't let a man raise a hand to you, 'cause he'll never stop."

"Did he—did he kill her?"

"I don't know," she said, taking a quick swallow of juice. Her eyes had gone so hard, so quick. "No one would ever say. An accident, that's all I heard. I went to the funeral, it was back home. It'd been almost three years by then. My sisters were so disappointed I didn't bring you." She leaned toward me, smiling again.

"They didn't care you didn't have a father. Family's family," she repeated. "We kind of made up slowly, me and dad. But I still miss her sometimes. Regina."

We sat in the quiet for a minute. Outside, a woman called something in Spanish, and a child replied. My mother's eyes looked unfocused, her mouth pursed to one side. She blinked and reached for her glass

"You been to church?"

"No. They don't like lesbians, remember?"

"Skyler," she scolded, but her eyes were amused.

"And last I heard, they didn't feel that much better about women in general. Have you been?" I returned.

Her jaw dropped and then she laughed, slapping

me on the leg.

"I'll see you in Hell."

The phone rang from the hall.

"It's Sunday, for Christ's sake. Who's that?" she demanded, heading toward the hall, cigarette in hand.

"It's God," I quipped. "He's checking to see if you went to church."

She was laughing as she picked up the phone.

"Hello, who is this?"

My ma. There was no one else like her.

"Gloria, hello, how are you?"

I stretched out on the bed. On her dresser I could see the same perfume she always used. Jean Naté. Though it wasn't perfume exactly. What did they call it? After Bath Splash. Not that you could smell anything over the cigarettes. I think it just made her feel feminine or sexy or something. The smoke was really getting to me, though. My eyes and throat were starting to burn. I picked up her juice and took a swallow.

It was halfway down my throat before I realized and by then my throat was on fire. I choked and coughed and some of it spilled out of my mouth onto the floor. I didn't care. There was probably just enough juice to give it color, but it was bourbon.

And suddenly I was far away and real close up, all at once, and a voice in my head was saying, *Put the glass down, put the glass down, put it down*, because I wanted to smash it. To throw it and smash it and watch it break. To have it leave my hand with all the force I could manage. Damn it, God damn it, God fucking damn it.

"Okay, Gloria, I'll see you tomorrow," I heard my mother.

I got off the bed as she came back in. For half a second her face looked puzzled as she realized something was wrong. I was still holding the glass.

"This isn't juice," I said, my voice strangling itself in my throat. "It isn't juice," I heard myself wailing. "You're drinking and you've been out of the hospital for a week! You're drinking and you've been out of the hospital for one fucking week!" and all the while that voice was saying,

Down, Put it down, Put down the glass.

"Don't you speak to me like that!" she yelled, outraged. And slightly drunk. "Who the hell do you think you are?"

"I'm your daughter!" I was screaming like I had never screamed. "And you're a drunk! Every single night, Ma!" I was sobbing now on top of the screaming, my voice unrecognizable, pure, animal pain forcing itself into words. "You come home from work and drink yourself into a stupor, every goddamn night—"

That was when she hit me. My little mother. She raised her hand and hit me in the face. And I took the glass and smashed it into the floor, the liquid flew upwards, splashing on the walls, shards of glass in slow motion catching the light as they separated, so many from one, I did it, I smashed it, and then there was silence.

"I gotta get out of here," I sobbed, pushing past her. She didn't try to stop me.

For the second time that afternoon, I ran.

FIVE

I lay on my bed staring at the wall, still out of breath. There had been something so wild and reckless in my heart the whole way home, pushing me faster and faster as if I could out distance grief, like I could arrive home before it and pound up the stairs, Steed slung across my shoulder, and slam the door in its hungry face.

But of course it didn't work that way. It's hard to be reckless lying on your bed, and the wildness had left for parts unknown. Which left me two choices: that sadness that I can never see the bottom of, or going numb. I knew my drug of choice. I slept.

I woke to the smell of food. Onions and garlic and oregano. God, I was hungry. I sat up slowly, feeling thick and slightly dazed and knowing something was wrong. My room looked okay, my three big windows, my blue milk-crate book shelves, a Take Back The Night poster, my Richenbacher bass—Ricki, we called her—leaning back against the wall like all she needed was a cigarette to complete the pose, and lots of flyers tacked up. Flyers announcing us, Minor Disturbance, for different gigs. My jeans and sneakers lay abandoned on the floor. And Diane Frasier's purse.

Oh yeah. My life of crime. And then my mother. No wonder I felt like I'd been bludgeoned.

I got up and stumbled into the kitchen. It was painted a shade of mauve that usually I liked, but not right now. It was too nice, too lesbian, too home. It made me mad. I sank into a chair and wanted some food. The clock read 5:15 PM. The co-op had already closed. God-fucking-shit-head damn it.

Jaye appeared and stirred whatever delightfulness she was preparing on the stove. Can I have some? I practiced in my head a few times. Hey, Jaye, you got enough for two?

Forget it. I was too hungry and too humiliated.

"Nice outfit," Jaye commented conversationally, referring to my underweared state.

"Shut up," I mumbled with a little too much bite.

Jaye put down her wooden spoon and turned around to face me.

"Hey, you okay?"

"Yeah, I'm fine," I snapped. And I realized I hadn't eluded grief at all. It got me while I slept, waiting patiently for me until I'd made myself vulnerable, and then curling up all cozy in my heart.

I swallowed hard.

"No," I said, in a calmer tone of voice. "Everything sucks."

"Your mom?"

I nodded 'cause I couldn't speak.

"Wanna have dinner?" she offered. "Peppers and tofu sausage?"

It was that easy. The kindness was always what got me, like water that always finds the crack. Jaye could see what was on my side of the fridge. Nothing.

I swallowed again and spoke carefully. "Thanks. Yes. Let me go put my jeans on."

When I returned she'd dished up our dinner. Beautiful slices of red and green peppers, over fresh pasta glistening with olive oil and speckled with herbs. There were candles lit in two purple glass holders and the dinner plates were deep blue with green leaves. From Crate and Barrel. Her parents.

They weren't rich, I mean middle class isn't the same as rich-rich, but still. To me it was usually the same difference.

I tell you one thing I learned though, being friends with Jaye. Money really doesn't buy happiness. Her parents were divorced, her dad had been a coke addict, her step-father had sexually abused her and her mom didn't really believe her. Money came sometimes, but only sometimes, and it never came easy.

"Sorry I'm such a bitch," I said, but I couldn't look up. Sorry is hard for me.

"Bitch all you want," she said easily. "You put up

with my PMS every month." She gave a short laugh and loaded up her fork. We ate in silence for a minute. The food was so good it hurt.

"She been drinking again?" Jaye asked in her straight-up Jaye way.

I nodded and pushed a pepper across my plate. Jaye was waiting. It was my turn. She wouldn't ask any-more, it was up to me. I looked up. Her hair was short and spikey, her blunt face both tough and open. Jay'd been an alcoholic, too. Her fourth anniversary of being sober had just passed.

"She's killing herself," I replied, getting in deeper with each word.

Jaye put down her fork. "Yeah. She really might drink herself to death."

I pushed the pepper back to the other side. It was hard enough being friends. I wasn't going to cry.

"Listen," said Jaye, "I'm not going to press, but I wish you'd think about coming to meetings with me. I know you've said 'no' already, but it's really bad. It's really bad, Skyler. You shouldn't have to do this alone."

She didn't understand. No one ever got this part. But other people couldn't help. They weren't real enough somehow. People were outside things. The inside things were mine, where I lived, and I was really just a ghost in the other world. So it wouldn't help.

"Going to meetings isn't going to stop my mother from drinking," I said.

"Yeah, and that's the point. Nothing you do is go-ing to stop her," Jaye urged.

Easy for you to say. Your dad's off drugs, I wanted to snap. It was a nasty thought, defensive and wounding, and I wished I hadn't had it.

"I don't want to go. It won't help."

"Okay," she smiled, "but if you ever change your mind . . ."

We ate some more in a friendly silence. Jaye could keep things light. Like she was pretty intense, but on her own terms. Maybe it's a Virgo thing, I don't know, but I se-cretly admire it. She always gets the details right in this graceful kind of way, because she's living that far. It must be a Virgo thing. Of course, that lets me off the hook nicely, being a lowly Gemini, since you can't change what you're born.

So we chatted about the band, and Jaye's fundraising job, and feminism and girls. And I realized I hadn't had a chance to daydream about Judith's mouth all day.

When I got back to my room I still didn't have a chance, because there on the floor was Diane's purse. All right, first things first. I flipped on the radio. Then I sat on the floor and unceremoniously upended the bag.

The contents made some noise but were basically well-behaved as they fell out, except for a tube of lipstick that started rolling away. I plucked it up and examined the color. Kind of cinnamon-pink, nothing too garish, from The Body Shop. That's one thing I'll never get. I mean, it's good not to torture animals and all, but if you're gonna look at the world politically, you have to include women, too, which to me means saying 'fuck you' to femininity. And at least making an effort to love our bodies the way they really are. The beauty thing's such a desperate treadmill and there's no way for us to win. Why don't we just blow the whole thing off—or up—or something.

Oh, well. Exhibit 1, lipstick.

Exhibit 2. Her wallet. A driver's license and a modest number of credit cards. There was a picture, too, a small black and white photo from a photo booth like they have at the old Woolworth's. Diane and a man holding a little blond girl, all of them laughing. Jonathan and Chloe, I assumed. Revere Beach, someone had written on the back and dated it two summers ago. He was good-looking, with dark wavy hair and kind eyes. But the kid was adorable, a little laughing cherub. Chloe. I put the picture back in her wallet.

I opened the money part and blinked. There was a fat stack of bills. I blinked again. The bank machine, of course. I started counting. It was all twenties. I was holding $300. Unbelievable. Should I make it be Exhibit 3? What should I do with it? Was it mine to spend? My mind began to drift into a haze of consumptive fantasies. Black Levi's, some CD's, God, the food I could get, or I could keep Ricki in bass string for awhile . . . I was going to have to think about this. I carefully put the money back in the wallet.

Exhibit 4. A plastic bag full of. . . Holy shit. The bag was filled with drugs. Pills, all kinds, sorted into little bags. I slowly put it down. What the hell was going on? And what the hell was I going to do with these?

Exhibit 5 was her address book. I flipped through it. This would probably come in handy, if I could figure out how. I couldn't just randomly call people, Hello, you don't know me but I stole Diane Frasier's purse because I think she was murdered and do you have any information about that? I sighed. Then I noticed a scrap of paper stuck in the front. "April Gordon" was written on it and a long distance phone number. I realized almost immediately that the handwriting wasn't Diane's. Was it important? Who knew? I stuck it back in the book.

Exhibit 6 was a small brown bag containing a box of hair dye. There was a receipt in the bag for the Shop Mart in J. P. Where the ATM was. The date was today at 12:14 AM. So last night, in other words. According to the receipt, she'd bought two boxes. Ah, but there had been an empty box in her trash can.

Exhibit 7 was a large blue stick-um with directions written on it. I started to read them to see if I could orient myself and it was easy. *Huntington Ave. to Centre St.,* it began. So Brookline to Jamaica Plain. I read it all the way through. I didn't know the exact street but it was near the pond and not far from my house. *173 Harken St. Blue house, purple trim.*

Exhibit 8 was the pills I'd grabbed from her medicine chest. They were indeed identical. Through the orange plastic I could see shiny green and white capsules piled up to the cotton plugs. The label read The Bridden Family Pharmacy, Wellesley. *Take one capsule once a day in the morning,* the instructions instructed. *Fluoxetine hydrochloride—20 mg* and a doctor's name were written at the bottom.

Exhibit 9 was her checkbook. Current balance: $3,573.26. Not bad. Her checks were printed with the message Pro-woman=Pro-choice in bright red. Go for it, Diane.

Exhibit 10 was everything else lumped together. A couple of tampons whose wrappers had seen whiter days, a comb, two blue pens, a bottle of Advil, a flowered scrunchy, some Barney bandaids—and another bottle of pills?

I compared them next to Exhibit 8. Yup. They were a set. But I'd only found two in the medicine chest. So one of them must have already been in her purse. Three unopened bottles of exactly the same pills?

I also found the bag Amy had given me at the restaurant. It held two large carob-chip cookies, if you can put macrobiotic and cookie in the same sentence. They actually weren't bad, though. I munched and flicked off the radio. All they'd played was boys and my head was starting to hurt.

All right, what did I actually know?

Diane Frasier. She was dead. So was her husband Jonathan. She had a four-year-old daughter. She had bought two bottles of hair coloring after midnight. In J. P., even though she lived in Brookline. She had then gone to the bank machine, also in J. P., and been upset because she wanted more money even though it gave her $300.

Then a man who was a doctor came in and made threatening noises about her daughter, and references to the police finding drugs in her car. Then she'd gone home and . . . dyed her hair?

Also, the same or a different doctor had gone to her house today with a crew of obnoxious young men in search of her will.

She had in her possession three unopened bottles of fluoex-whatever and she died from a prescription drug overdose.

She also had a large bag full of presumably illegal drugs.

Now I had a bag full of presumably illegal drugs. What the hell was I supposed to do with it? I had a terrible urge to hide it, and I was going to be fidgety until I did. I stood up and stuck it under my shirt. Jaye was in the bathroom running water for a bath. I darted into the kitchen and looked around for inspiration. There was a crumbled bag from The Bagel Bakery on the floor of the pantry. I opened it with a quick snap and dropped my contraband in. Then I shoved it into the bottom bin on my side of the fridge and propped two soft, sprouting onions on top of it. That should do for a couple of days.

Back in my room, I put the rest of her things back in her purse. This was my conclusion. Chances were good that she had visited the house on Harken St., where she had probably never been before, ergo the instructions. Afterwards, she had stopped at the store . . . Something clicked in my brain. The hair dye in her trash can. The model on the box had been blond. But Diane had brown hair. I fished out the receipt. Yup, *Born Blonde Hair Color*. And the box that was left in her purse was brown. So she had dyed her hair blond, and then was going to dye it back? Had she bought the brown box in case she didn't like herself as a blond?

Wait a minute. The little girl. Chloe. She was blond in the picture. The brown dye could have been for her.

That settled it. Diane Frasier was about to make a run for it. How or who or why, I didn't know and I couldn't think about it anymore. Judith hadn't called and my mother was probably passed out instead of sleeping and Chloe Frasier was in danger. Everything had gotten way too scary and I'd had enough.

I took off my clothes and went back to sleep.

SIX

The co-op opens at 8 o'clock and me and Steed were there at 7:56 AM. I wasn't taking any chances. I had my list, my money and my backpack. I was buying food.

Waiting with me was another dyke who I didn't know, but we grinned and nodded, as befitted members of the tribe. There was another woman too, with a little girl in a stroller. The kid was seriously cute: tiny corn rows, fat little arms, and a smile of pure delight. We played wave hi, hide your face and giggle, which her mother observed with tolerant amusement. Finally, at 8:01 AM, a white guy with dreadlocks opened the door. This guy annoys me. I think his name's Billy. He always wears these grungy tie-dyes with lots of orange and purples. I'm talking ugly. I can't help it, I have this really critical edge sometimes, and I look at him and I want to say: It's almost the year 2000. By the time you were born the yuppies had already taken over Haight-Ashbury. Cut your hair, change your clothes and get a life. To top it all off, he always says hi to me in this really slavish way, like if he could get the approval of a man-hating lesbian, his existence would be complete. He also figured out my name from my checks.

"Hi, Skyler," he groveled, as I brought up the rear. Oh, what a day it was for him. He could hold the door for two dykes and a woman of color with a baby.

Go commit suicide, I wanted to growl. You're responsible. It's all your fault. And you'll never make up for it. Never, do you hear me, never! Ha ha ha! The evil laughter rang in my head as I said hi back. Yeah, I said hi. I always do. I just can't be that mean to ignore him.

I pondered Billy as I methodically made my way through the store. It was the way he oozed guilt without any effort toward action. What was he actually doing to stop racism or violence against women? Huh? I dropped cream cheese into my basket. They made their own bagels here and they were good. Was he raising money for the Rape Crisis Hotline, or doing civil disobedience for welfare moms, or destroying pornography? No. The spaghetti sauce I liked was on sale, as was the organic broccoli. It was almost the same price as the regular. I wondered what Billy was like in his personal life, with women, but I backed away from that one fast. Ick, ick, ick. And finally a yummy treat for my troubles. A day-old honey sticky bun or a chocolate chip brownie? I went with the brownie and made my mental calculations one more time. $25 ought to do it.

And it did, with $1.26 to spare. Billy was nowhere in sight. I smiled at the woman behind the counter.

When I got home, I left Steed on the street while I went up to unload the groceries. I had to leave again in a few minutes for an extremely disagreeable appointment at the Department of Employment and Training. In plain English, the unemployment office. They wanted to "review" my Worksearch Activity Log. In other words, they didn't like me and they didn't believe me. I was glad I'd bought the brownie. I was gonna need it.

"You list your occupation as 'musician'," said Ms. Allen, hesitating just enough before the last word to let me know what she thought of it. "However, your employment record doesn't show any paid employment as a musician."

The emphasis was definitely on the paid.

There was a small silence while we both sized each other up. She was ugly. Let me rephrase that. What life had done to her and what she'd done to herself was all over her face. Literally. That self-satisfied self-hatred called femininity. And I wanted to scrub it all off.

All right, I felt stupid and humiliated and it made me mad. I tried to replace the scrubbing with a gentler image. Priestesses. At the Temple. She has never been attended to so sweetly. Like a child soothed by a lullaby, she lets them. They quietly disrobe her, the tight skirt, the polyester blouse, the bra straps digging into her shoulders, the panty hose smelling of stale sweat. They gasp as each new horror is revealed, her contorted feet and torturous shoes, her strange fingernails, her stubbled legs and underarms, the bizarre cloth fitted around her groin, exchanging glances of bewildered concern. Her face is gently bathed, and the smelly pastes are washed away. Her hair, too, is cleansed in a basin of water. They have never seen hair this color, they whisper to themselves. And the texture, the way it retains its shape, but the water seems to help. She looks a little better now that her flesh has been freed and she doesn't smell so strange. The Crone is called and her two assistants. They lay her on a bed of fresh linen and with skilled fingers rub deep into her muscles.

To no avail, the Crone tells them all later. We could feel no spirit in her flesh. She is dead except she breathes. I've seen nothing like it.

They all shake their heads.

She won't eat, says one of the mothers. She keeps jabbing her legs and hips and making a terrible face. Why would she hate her— and here she uses a word for which there is no translation. It means fecundity, joy, softness, and fat. It means mother and lover and silky and sacred. Why would she hate it so?

I, says one of the bold, young Amazons, would love her— and here there is another word, almost the same as the first except for the inflection. A pun. The women laugh. The word means clitoris and bring the Goddess forth, both noun and verb.

It'll be many seasons, sighs the Crone, before she's ready for that.

"Well?" demanded Ms. Allen.

"I'm sorry?" I was forced to ask. Her tight little mouth got tighter.

"You're collecting unemployment for a job at *The Jamaica Plain Tab*?"

"Correct," I nodded non-committally.

"And what did you do there?" She was bored and angry and she couldn't breathe and her feet must be killing her, and since she couldn't figure it out, she took it out on everyone around her.

"I was a production assistant."

"You have three years of college," she said, rustling through my file.

Yeah, and my underwear's blue, my period should

begin next week, and I floss my teeth every night. It's none of your goddamn business.

"What was your major?"

Lesbiology, I wanted to say. Yes, the study of lesbians. I did my research on patterns of vulvic pleasure. I considered a minor in Post Traumatic Stress Syndrome—I am a rape survivor, so it seemed natural—but I decided against it. I minored in feminist activism, including the usual field study in rabble rousing and suicide by collective process.

"Communications," I mumbled.

"We need to change this," she said like she was talking to a four-year-old. She picked up a red pen with her red painted fingernails, having to do everything sideways to accommodate them. A quick slash and it was all over. Musician, sliced right through the middle, corrected with "newspaper production" in that same red ink.

Fuck you. I looked over her desk while she read over my Worksearch Activity Log. That's where you have to fill in a little chart with the names and dates of all the "acceptable worksearch activities" you've done to get a job. She had a folding plastic picture frame with pastel 3-D flowers decorating the border. One side had a girl, the other a boy. They looked exactly like her, in a gender appropriate way. Life is scary.

"You had an interview," she said, looking up.

Surprise, surprise, even losers like me get job interviews once in a while.

"Any word?" her tone just this side of sarcasm.

No, I'm sitting here because I can't think of a livelier way to spend my final twenty-four hours of unemployment.

"No," I sighed.

Her eyes lingered on my hair, and then my clothes. I swear she shook her head. Hey, not everybody wants to look like you. When I go to an interview, everything is neat, clean and, yes, announces my gender clearly, all right?

"Well," she said, her mouth struggling into a smile like gravity was this huge strain. "Everything seems to be in order. Make sure to keep filling in your Activity Log."

"Thanks," I mimicked her tone as I got up.

"You only have six weeks of unemployment left," she added, just for laughs.

I could see her in the junior high girls' locker room. Can you believe that shirt she's wearing? And her hair's so greasy you could cook with it. All within earshot of the intended victim. I had this terrible urge to pour her Diet Sprite over her moussed do. The Leaning Tower of Hair.

But I just ignored her. It's the best thing to do in these situations. She got off on nastiness when she was twelve and nothing's changed since then. But it made me mad that she had power then and she had power now. Then it was over the girls who weren't pretty, or didn't have the right clothes, and now it was the people who stood quietly in line with a resigned desperation, their mouths determined against the shame.

I was glad to get out. The natural light was a relief and Steed looked fine and ready for action. I'm not a failure, I'm a lesbian, I chanted to myself, as if truth lay in repetition. I wasn't paying such good attention to traffic as I rode, especially considering how fast I was going, but I didn't care. I just didn't care.

I played my bass the rest of the afternoon. Me and Ricki go way back. The summer I was fourteen I lied about my age, got a job at Dunkin' Doughnuts, saved all my money and bought my bass guitar. My mother thought it was a little strange, but didn't really care. I didn't play loud, just a lot.

I like music 'cause it's just me. I did all the hard stuff first, my fingers stretching up and down the neck in a quick succession of warm ups, then working out the bass part for a song Amy wrote. After that I just sat against the wall and played. Sometimes the music just moves right through you, coaxing you to come with it, and little by little I followed, separating myself from my pain. There was respite in the separation, there always is, and I can just breathe while the music does the rest. I could see my mother, the disease that was sucking her dry like a hemorrhage no one could stop and my grief flowing right behind, God, there had to be an end to it somewhere, I wanted to wail, and the music kept coming, a heartbeat that would never stop, resonating in blood and bone and I closed my eyes and felt it.

SEVEN

The house was blue with purple trim, just like Diane's directions said. 157 Harken Street. It was big too, with a great view and an obviously amazing garden, even this early in the season. Tall flowers of speckled pink and peach and yellow were placed generously around a curving brick path. There was a wrought iron railing going up the steps and a lazy looking porch swing by a blooming vine. And, hip hip hooray, their names were on the mail box. Joan and Nathan Strauss.

I had gone through Diane's address book page by page, but none of the entries had the Harken Street address. So not only did I have no idea what I was going to say, I didn't know who I was going to say it to.

I held my breath and rang the bell. It was around six, so I was hoping someone would be home.

"Coming!" I heard a woman's voice, then her footsteps. I swallowed and ran a hand through my hair. What there was of it.

The door opened and we blinked at each other. She was white, short and pretty in a sharp kind of way, with dark hair piled neatly on her head. She was wearing a long, slim skirt with an oversized bright blue jacket and perfunctory make-up.

"Yes?" she prompted, still holding the doorknob, her wrist circled by big blue stones. She was smiling but she was also ready to slam the door.

"I'm a friend of Diane Frasier's," I heard myself say. "I was wondering if I could talk to you for a few minutes."

Her smile ended. She didn't get angry, but there was something behind the sudden poker face, something in her eyes. Fear, I thought.

"Diane Frasier," she repeated, looking at me harder.

Maybe I was being paranoid, but if someone had been murdered, there was no point in advertising my name.

"My name's Julie Cavanaugh," I said, choosing the name of the first girl I kissed. In seventh grade, on the way home from school. Julie, Julie, where are you now?

"Yeah, all right, come in," she said, holding open the

door. She looked worried but she definitely wasn't one to lose her cool.

I stepped inside. The hall had a really high ceiling and dark wood molding, carved into flowers at the corners. I could see the living room, with crimson upholstery on the couch and chairs, and a brick fireplace painted white. From the back of the house, I heard a door open and a man's voice. A second later a small child came running around the corner, dressed in Gap Kids kinda clothes.

"Mommy mommy mommy!" she sang, throwing her arms around her mother's legs. She had brown skin and black, black hair cut in a straight line of bangs across her forehead.

"Lisa," her mother sang back, hoisting the kid up off the floor.

"Daddy bought cookies for me and Jenny," she told her mother in a confidential tone, glancing shyly at me. I wondered if she was adopted or if Nathan was a person of color.

Joan laughed and put her down. "Daddies are like that. Now listen, I want to hear all about your day, but I need to talk to this lady and I also need to get dressed for the reception. So that's a lot to do. If you want to help, you could play upstairs or out on your swing set while I talk to Julie."

"Is she a girl or a boy?" Lisa asked, swinging on Joan's hand and looking at me directly.

You're never too young to know the importance of gender, I thought with a sigh. At least it was an honest question. Give her a few years. Something contemptuous and cruel would start creeping in, about the same time that "queer," "lezzie," and "fag" started being insults. Some things never change. If you can't tell, why does it matter? was my standard response. Some kids got so frustrated. It wasn't their fault, I guess, that the world was forming their brains into absolute hierarchies of categories, but I could see the future in their questions and I didn't like it.

"She's a woman," Joan replied matter-of-factly, with an amused smile that included me.

"When's Jenny coming?" Lisa pleaded, still tugging

on her arm.

"How about a little separation anxiety, kiddo? Show your mother you love her? Most kids, when their parents go out, they cry, they scream. But my daughter. The only four year old in America who can't wait for the baby-sitter."

Lisa's got a crush, I wanted to tease.

"Soon, Lisa, okay? Come on. Go play. Go bug your father. I've gotta talk to Julie."

Lisa considered for a moment, and then ran off around the corner where she'd come from.

"Nat?" she called, as an afterward. "Don't give her cookies until she's had dinner. Nat?" She rolled her eyes. "One minute," she said, holding up a commanding finger. She followed after Lisa in what I assumed was the direction of the kitchen.

In my unsupervised sixty seconds, I had time to glance over a small table that held mail and a telephone. There was pad of message paper beside the phone. I pulled a used sheet lose and tucked it quickly into my back pocket. I didn't have time to notice much besides a garden catalog and a letter postmarked in Maryland. Her steps were returning so I retreated from the table and tried to look innocent and bored.

"Now," she said, motioning me into the living room. "What can I do for you?"

She sat on the antique couch, stretching her arms out along the back of it. What she lacked in height she made up for in body language.

I sat on a matching chair and wished I'd worn nicer clothes. I took a breath and dropped my jaw, not knowing what was going to come out.

"Did you hear that Diane—about her death?" stumbled from my mouth.

Joan nodded. "I read it in the paper."

"I didn't know her well, but I don't think it was suicide. I mean, I don't know what I think, but there's something else going on, and I thought maybe you might—I mean—" the words were piling up like rear-ended cars on a freeway. Focus, Skyler.

"From what I understand, she was here the night she was killed."

"What makes you think she was killed?" Her tone was light, but I didn't believe it. Not quite. Something in her body language. She was too still, like she was holding on too hard, and she wasn't breathing enough.

"She got in an argument with someone—a man—a tall guy, he was a doctor. I don't know his name," I was watching her carefully and had the feeling it was mutual.

She shrugged. "Listen, I can't really help you much. Diane Frasier was a client of mine. I'm a landscape architect and she was thinking about hiring me to do some work for her. She stopped by to return some gardening books I'd lent her."

At midnight on a Saturday night? Yeah, right.

"I didn't have any kind of a personal relationship with her. Sorry," she finished.

"She didn't say where she was going next?"

"No."

"And you don't know anything about the guy she was fighting with?"

"Probably somebody she was dating. I wouldn't worry about it," she shrugged.

That's exactly when I would worry about it, I wanted to protest. *Crimes against women are crimes of proximity: it's the men we know who do it to us,* ran through my head like a mantra. Then the statistics, like a feminist rosary, worn smooth by repetition, only it was my heart instead of plastic beads.

"So I can't really help you," she said again, getting to her feet.

It was obvious the interview was at an end. I stood up, too.

"Thanks anyway," I mumbled, as she herded me toward the door.

"Hey, I'm sorry about your friend," she said placing her hand on my arm for a second as I crossed the threshold.

"Thanks," I mumbled as she shut the door. My last sight was of little Lisa standing on the stairs wearing a huge floppy hat and giggling. Cute kid.

Steed got me home in under ten minutes, and I was shaking my head the whole way. I just didn't believe her. Diane Frasier had decided to leave in a hurry and something happened Saturday night that had made her decide.

I set Steed down in the hall and unlocked the door. The answering machine wasn't blinking. In other words, Judith hadn't called. I sighed and wheeled Steed to her royal quarters. I had one more Diane-related task, and then I was going to have to take matters into my own hands. Judith needed a reminder that I existed. The cost to my pride was fast losing pace to the widening stress fracture in my heart. No, it wasn't broken yet, but I was going to have to call her.

EIGHT

I pulled Diane's handbag out from under my bed and fished around for her address book. The slip of scrap paper was still in the front, where I'd returned it. "April Gordon," it read, with a phone number in the 215 area code. I reached into my back pocket and removed the message paper I'd swiped from the Strausses. I'd noticed originally that "April Gordon" was in a handwriting that wasn't Diane's. So the question was, was it Joan's or Nathan's.

"Nat," read the first message, in a quick, clipped script that had to be Joan's. "Bob needs you to call him re: Steven's case."

In the same writing but a different pen were the words, "Arriving 2:53, Continental #1205."

Then came, "Gail—reminding about parents' meeting, wants us to call."

I read through the rest of their messages, written in that domestic shorthand that's the same in every house. Missing nouns, mismatched cases, implying both speed and intimacy. I held the April slip next to the Strausses'. Chalk one up for the home team. It looked like a perfect match. Joan Strauss had given Diane the number.

I flopped onto the bed while I thought up a plan. What did I want to find out from April Gordon? Okay, think, Gabriel. Round up all the possibilities and let's see what we've got.

All right. Let's pretend everyone's telling the truth. Diane went to J. P. to return some gardening books. She left the Strausses' and then engaged in unknown activities until I met her at twelve. Then the doctor made threatening noises, she went home, dyed her hair, and committed suicide. The next morning Fascist Fuzz Boy and Friends were rifling through her papers because for legitimate, if oblique reasons, they wanted her will. And her purse was stuffed with uppers, downers and in-betweeners because . . . she'd found them on the street and didn't want any small children to get a hold of them.

Sure, that's really likely.

The most obvious angle was the drugs. The woman's husband dies, leaving her with one small child and one large house. She has a job but maybe she likes the advantages of a two-career income. Maybe it's the style to which she has become accustomed. She's got a connection—maybe the Evil Doctor—and she decides to try her hand at selling drugs.

Yeah, and then maybe she changes her mind. Maybe she decides it's a career with a glass ceiling of cement block and iron bars. Or maybe the job description changed to include activities she wasn't interested in. And then termination ended in death.

Did upper middle class single moms deal drugs? Drugs like these? Maybe she was a courier. Maybe the Doctor et al told her when to go where, carrying a yellow umbrella and a secret code word, and all she had to do was deliver the goods for a nice leg up on the ol' mortgage payments. Nobody would suspect a woman like Diane Frasier. She'd be perfect.

And then she'd wanted out. But she knew too much. He'd threatened her, tried to strong arm her with Chloe. She'd been ready to disappear into the mist, but she hadn't moved fast enough.

I sat up, excited. I was on to something and my heartbeat was keeping pace with my thoughts. But where did the Strausses fit into it, who was April G., and why were the Bad People looking for her will? I couldn't do anything more with the Strausses for now, or the Bad People, but Ms. G . . . I had an idea.

I sat at my desk for a few minutes, working on a script, my pencil flying furiously. Then I read it over with a grin. Cleverness appeals to me, even when it's my own. Of course, my bright ideas tend to look a bit dimmer in retrospect, but I never remember that until it's too late.

I grabbed the phone and the phone book from the hall and went back into my room. I flipped quickly through the first few pages, those pages I never need. International calls, those rate charts that tell you that, surprise surprise, long distance is cheapest at 2 AM. Ah, there it was. A line drawing of the US of A, divided up into area codes like latter-day political protectorates. Goddess forbid they should do anything as useful as list them in numerical order. But I found it. 215 was in the southeast corner of Pennsylvania, including Philadelphia. I'd never been there, but at least I knew it was the same time zone.

"Here goes," I said out loud as I pushed the little touch tone buttons.

One ring. Two. Of course, I was half hoping no one was home, but of course someone was.

"Hello?" said a female voice. A sweet voice, considerate and even, the kind of voice you'd want around if you busted yourself and needed stitches.

"Hello, may I speak to April Gordon?" I asked in that friendly, professional tone the sales people and receptionists use.

"Speaking."

I started reading at an even pace. "Good evening, Ma'am. My name is Marcia Evans and I'm calling from *Time* magazine. We're doing a survey on how Americans feel about illegal drugs. The survey should take five minutes or less, so if you could give us that much time?"

"All right," she replied.

"The first few questions are demographic. Are you between the ages of eighteen and thirty?" I paused slightly, but she didn't respond. "Thirty and forty-five?"

"Yes," she said.

"And is your total household income less than 20 thousand dollars; between 20 and 40 thousand dollars; between and 40 and 60 thousand dollars—" oh, the excitement was rising now, "—between 60 and 80 thousand; between 80 and 100 thousand—"

"Yes," she answered easily.

"And are you married, single, widowed or divorced?"

Except none of those categories ever seem to fit me. I usually write in "lesbian" on forms, and draw a little box which I check off. The dyke version would have a collection to choose from. Check whichever apply: dating, considering, committed, non-monogamous, monogamous, celibate (by choice), single (not by choice), confused, none of your business, and categories are patriarchal.

"Married," she said, that smooth voice still attentive and kind.

"And do you have any children, Ma'am?"

There was silence. Not just an absence of words, but an absence of breath. I thought she'd hung up.

"Hello?"

"I'm sorry," she replied, her voice gone high and tight. "I had a child. She's gone. She died."

Grief cracked her voice wide open on the last word, and a soft sobbing found its way through.

"I'm so sorry," I said, stunned. I'd just stumbled through her defenses like they were paper.

"I'm really sorry," I repeated, feeling like a buffoon.

"I just don't understand. I wanted her so badly and I loved her so much—" she was begging someone for an answer, a stranger on the end of the phone.

"I'm sure you did," I said and meant every word.

"I'm sorry," she replied, as if her grief had been a long, hard road and these words her final destination. "Maybe it's just that she never got a chance."

"I had a cousin who disappeared," I offered slowly, hoping she could meet me half-way. "Grace. She was named after Grace Kelly. It was months before they found her body. And still nobody knows what happened." And we don't like to think about it, no, we don't.

"That's horrible," she said, her voice firmer, putting her sorrow away again. "How old was she?"

"Sixteen."

"Horrible," she answered, absorbing her own pictures of Grace's death. I could get lost in here, too. I didn't know my cousins well, they lived too far away and family relations were still too strained. Grace had long brown hair and narrow hips that swayed slow when she showed the rest of us how to dance.

"Like this," she suggested, her sex still just this side of innocent. All the teenage cousins laughed and laughed and they all tried. Me and the others under ten, "the babies" they called us, but not meanly, watched giggling from

Grace's bed. Later they put lipstick on us and all our mothers screamed, "Jesus, Joseph, and Mary, what the hell did you do to those kids?" Twice a year they sent me clothes, a big cardboard box of cast-offs that smelled faintly like them, like the too-sweet perfume made for teenage girls.

And then Grace disappeared and still all I could do was pray. That it had been quick. The life of a girl almost woman, reduced to prayers for a quick death.

"Yeah, it's horrible," my voice stripped clean of any pretense. "Listen, let's just forget the survey. I need to take a break. I'm sorry to disturb you and bring all this back."

"I'm sorry, too. It's all right. Thanks for listening," she said, her voice even again.

"Take care of yourself, Mrs. Gordon," I added.

"You do the same," she said like she meant it.

I lay my head down before I put the receiver back. The dial tone is always so final. There was a voice, a human connection, and then nothing. My hand finally found the cradle and then there was silence.

I didn't have to call Judith. She called me. She was apologetic and sweet and unequivocal.

"I can't be in a relationship right now, Skyler. I just can't. I've been in relationships for twelve years straight and I need to be alone. I'm sorry. I'm sorry we kissed. I mean, I don't regret it," she laughed, "but I'm sorry if it's more painful for you now."

"Oh," was all I could say.

"But you'll still be my friend, won't you? I think you're great, Skyler. Don't go away."

"No, I won't," I said calmly. Meanwhile, something cracked deep in my chest, something with sharp edges, and I felt it cut and then something leaking out, hot and liquid, filling me up and out my eyes, but I'd be damned if I let on. "I understand."

"Skyler, I'm sorry," and I could hear the concern in her voice but I didn't give a fuck.

"It's okay. Don't worry about it. We'll still be friends," I said, watching as each tear buffered my eyes from the stark planes and angles of the world for a second, before it fell and splattered on the desk. A kamikaze mission with no hope of victory, the war was already lost.

"Really?" she asked wistfully.

"Yeah, really," I said and changed the subject. Then I stayed on just long enough to show her that nothing was wrong.

When I hung up I didn't cry anymore. I kept thinking it would make me feel better, but nothing happened. So I went into the kitchen instead and, miracle of miracles, my brownie was waiting for me. It didn't drink; it couldn't get murdered; it wouldn't break my heart. Oh, Brownie, be mine, forever and ever, I begged as I devoured it.

NINE

I guess I'm not a moper. The house gets too small and I can't stand all my emotions crowding in around me. It's easier to leave, go out to a club or find someone to visit or walk until you don't know where you are. Otherwise, it hurts too much, and I'm not big on pain, especially my own.

When I was a kid I'd take off running. I'd go to the park and climb like a maniac or swing across the monkey bars, like I could scramble out of anger or burn myself clean of all attachments. My mother waited for my return, with time and place set free by alcohol. With every hour her speech took more effort for less effect and love goes rancid under the weight of disgust. Especially a child's love. When the other kids' parents called them in, I went home too, pretending somebody cared. If she was awake, I'd go into my room and slam the door as hard as I could. If she was snoring on the couch, I'd grab her arm and yank on it until she woke up. "Go to bed," I'd demand. "Don't sleep on the couch." I remember screaming that I hated her, but all she'd do was whimper and cover her head with her arm. Did I hit her once? Was it twice? Did I just want to or did I do it? I have this visceral memory of my hand coming down on her fleshy arm and my mother grunting. Like an animal. Like a pig, I thought. Or imagined.

Now I had Steed, who took me as far as I needed to go. There was still a little light in the sky, a few streaks of orange melting into a deepening blue. The cars had turned on their lights and so had Venus. The air was warm and moist and I wanted more. More air, more dark, more speed, more hard black top and soft evening sky, more songs from a saxophone player wailing on the corner, the hole in my chest was sucking in the world and nothing was enough to fill it. Cars streaked by, flat steel inches from my soft body, and I rode and rode and rode.

At 9 PM I was back at the Strausses', my mind emptied by endorphins. I stood across the street and watched for a minute. At least one thing had come clear during my ride: I probably wouldn't have another chance like this. I knew they were out for the evening, at a "reception" to be exact, and there was a sitter. The beloved Jenny. Who was probably twelve and watching tv while she did her algebra.

Breaking and Entering. Illegal in all fifty states. What if I didn't break anything? I crossed the street, steering clear of the most obvious spills of light. I checked around one more time. The house to the right was all dark. To the left, the glow from a television lit up the upstairs windows, but on the side farthest from the Strausses'. Behind me there were lights on in each of the houses. I tried to steady myself by remembering that when you're inside a lighted house, it's hard to see out when it's dark. And attitude is always 95 percent. Act like you're supposed to be doing what you're doing.

I took the curving path around to the back. It was darker by the side of the house in the protective shade of vegetation. The blossoms of a small tree shimmered silver-white in the shadows. Something animal takes over outside in the warm dark, something old and instinctive, you can feel your eyes getting bigger, your ears opening to the murmurs and rustlings, and you need to be part of it, but not for protection. You need to be part of it because it's all there is.

I paused in the shadows and heard my own breathing. I could see there were neighbors whose line of vision would include me. Just a question of whether anyone was looking. The ground had sloped downward, making the first floor windows too high to reach. The basement windows at ground level had iron grills over them, and there was no way I was going to attempt a break-in around front. That left the back door.

I turned the corner and tried to saunter casually, but it felt more like creeping. There was a light above the stairs, and the moment I turned the corner I was in it. I watched my feet as if they weren't my own. The back stairs were brick and around the door frame there was ivy growing, small leafed and dark. The door knob was smooth and cool and didn't budge under my hand. Nice try. I slipped back into the shadows. I needed a chance to think, but I couldn't do it here. I was still trespassing, which wasn't legal. I made my way back to the street and the open light of the city at night. The dark stayed behind, my senses shrinking to civilized proportions. It was a relief to reach the sidewalk, public property, paid for by my taxes.

Steed was waiting down the street and on my way to get her I had an idea. It was less than ten minutes back to my house, then a five minute layover, then ten minutes back... I was gambling for time now, since I didn't know how late the Strausses would stay out on a weeknight. But I could be back here by nine forty-five and finished by ten. It might work, I thought, grinning. It just might work.

Half an hour later I was at the Strausses' for the third time that evening, ringing the doorbell as legal as you please. I heard footsteps approach.

"Hello?" called a girls' voice.

"Hi, it's Julie," I replied confidently.

The door opened, with the safety chain limiting outside access to a crack. Smart kid. I wanted to pat her on the head for positive reinforcement: don't trust anyone.

"Hi, is Joan home yet?" I smiled and tried to act grown-up and professional.

"No," she replied. I could see her size me up: my black cowboy boots, blue jeans, red silk shirt and plush vest in a generic Native American rip-off pattern, with big silver buttons in the shape of cowboy hats. These last two garments came courtesy of Jaye's mom from a vacation in New Mexico. Jaye hadn't been home but I didn't think she'd mind me borrowing things she wouldn't be caught dead in.

I'd also firmly accessorized myself into the realm of the feminine, wearing practically every piece of jewelry that I owned. Hoop earrings from when I was twelve, fake-o silver bangles from about the same developmental stage, and a pin of a running horse that my first love gave me. Camouflaging my hair, or lack there of, was a black baseball hat turned backwards. And buried in a box in my closet I'd found the icing for this gender cake: a tube of lipstick last used in an undercover operation in college. We'd gained entry to a frat party and flushed cement down their toilet because they gang-raped women on a regular basis. At last count, their plumbing bill had exceeded $7,000. We considered the mission a success.

So anyway, there I stood, trying to feel easy and hip.

As for Jenny, I could see why Lisa liked her. She had creamy light brown skin and a saucy look in her eye. Her chin poked up while her mouth pulled sideways and the effect was both brave and endearing. She had a black bandanna tied in her hair and a shooting star tattooed on her cheek. I wondered what her mom said when she came home with that.

"I'm Julie Cavanaugh. Her intern? At work?" I prompted. "She was going to leave some stuff for me. It should be in a manila envelope, with my name on it?"

"She didn't mention it," Jenny said apologetically.

"Shit. She still at the reception?"

"Yeah," Jenny nodded.

I sighed and looked worried. "We've got a meeting tomorrow with one of our biggest clients. The design's finished but I was supposed to lay it all out nice and professional on the computer tonight. Joan cut this one a little too close," I laughed. "Do you think I could come in and look for it? It's probably right on the table or something." I mentally held my breath.

"Sure," she said, with a bored curl to her mouth. She undid the chain, and I was in.

"How's Lisa been tonight? Is she sleeping?" I asked, playing my last informational card.

"She's fine. Yeah, she's asleep," Jenny said. I could see what she was wearing now, a dress from the set of Little House on the Prairie, with zebra striped tights and black combat boots. She was an original.

"I'm on the phone," she said over her shoulder as she headed toward the kitchen.

"Oh, go ahead. I'll just poke around," I said, pausing at the hall table. It was too unreal, and being in character didn't help. I wanted to pay attention to the sensory data, just take a minute to smell the left-over scent of dinner, or listen to the radio in the next room letting loose a low volume of rap, but the fear was too big. Paying attention would probably mean throwing up. I decided to stick to dissociation, and started flipping through the now-opened mail. A fund-raising appeal from an environmental group, an American Express Gold Card Statement, the same gardening catalogs, and the personal letter, postmarked Maryland. I started reading.

Dear Joan,

I wanted to let you know how much I appreciated the flowers and phone calls when I was in the hospital. Hospitals are horrible places. They're supposed to be for healing, but they're too inhuman, and if I've realized one thing, it's this: I don't want to die in one.

Joan, what I've appreciated about our talks is your frankness. No one knows what to say, what to ask. Death is unmentionable in polite company. But it's there, like somebody wrecking havoc in the parlor, while everyone would rather ignore them. Of course, I may not die, but I still have to face it. I don't want to acknowledge it anymore than anyone else, but I still have to face it. It seems so, well, unnatural. I'm not even forty! Then I think of what you've been through. And I realize sometimes that, in a funny way, we all survive death, if we can just accept it, in all its pain and grief. Does this make any sense? Or is it the chemo talking again?

I'm looking forward to your visit.

I love you, Joan.

From Death's doorstep,
Alicia

I put the letter down and covered it gently with the other mail. It was too intimate, like I'd reached in and touched someone's spine when I'd only meant to pat them on the back. The reference to chemo must mean cancer. But what did she mean, "what you've been through?" Had Joan beat the odds against something? Had there been pain, dry heaves retching up what should nourish, had radiation stripped her clean of all protective animal covering, eyebrows, pubic tufts, that dark, thick pile I'd seen pinned to her head? I didn't want her to die. I didn't want anyone to die. How could her friend aim for acceptance?

But I'd have to think about it later. I shook my head to clear it and turned toward the stairs.

"Danielle!" Jenny shrieked, from the kitchen. "Girl, your mouth!"

The staircase was wide and graceful. The dark wood creaked underneath me but I didn't care since it was obvious Jenny didn't. At the top, a rug stretched in a slender strip down the hall floor, woven from some kind of reedy plant material dyed cobalt blue. Doors opened off the hall in symmetrical, opposite pairs, a neat Noah's Ark of rooms, three on each side.

The first one on my right looked like a guest room. There was a handmade quilt on the bed and wallpaper with a tiny floral pattern and it smelled vaguely like cleaning supplies. I left the door half open like I'd found it, mindful of where I put my fingerprints. Namely, no where.

Across the hall was someone's study. Shiny black steel bookcases were filled with orderly rows of books. *Ethics and Law,* said one hardback spine. *English Commonlaw In The American Colonies* was another juicy title. There was a big desk between the windows. I crossed over to it on a thick rug of dark green. I wanted to turn on the light but I was afraid. The desk was crowded but orderly, and a briefcase sat open on a chair. The light from the hall was too dim. My pupils were as big as they were gonna get. I was going to have to risk a light. Downstairs, Jenny shrieked again, and I jumped, my heart slamming my ribs in protest, like a prisoner pounding the bars with her demands. Sorry, heart, you're in for life. I took a breath to regain some calm, taking in the chemical smell of new carpet. Then, without further adieu, I switched on the desk lamp.

Nelson, Strauss and Wolfe, Attorneys at Law, read the raised print of letterhead. So, Nat was a lawyer. I knelt beside the briefcase and, pulling my hands inside my cuffs, began my rifling through a layer of silk. Clothes the well-dressed burglar simply shouldn't be without. The briefcase had a stack of manila folders, each label neatly typed, but none announcing Diane Frasier.

Ah, but what had we here. An unmarked folder, holding nothing except two newspaper clippings: the "Playwright Found Dead in Brookline Home" article that I'd seen in the restaurant and another one from *The Newton News.* That was a weekly paper, covering mostly west suburban stuff, and it came out on Mondays, which meant today. I read the article quickly. It repeated the same basic facts—the drug overdose, the suspected suicide, her accomplishments as a playwright—and then added a few new ones. She had taught theater at Northeastern University; she did a lot for the PTA; and the service was at 10 AM Wednesday at a funeral home in Brookline. The family was requesting that donations in her name be sent to the Reproductive Health Center at Boston General.

What else could I want? I could find out lots of stuff at the service, like maybe the whereabouts of Chloe. The article mentioned family. Maybe, I prayed, maybe, she was safely in the care of an aunt or a cousin or something. Maybe I was making all of this up.

Either way, I decided to quit while I was ahead. In sixty seconds I'd be out the door and on my way home. Relief was already beginning to work its relaxing wonders. I switched off the light just in time to see a sudden beam of light beside the house, accompanied by the sound of a nicely built engine.

The Strausses were home. Shit.

I had maybe two seconds to decide which door to run for and my body was already in flight, my heart in high gear. Gravity's so heavy in moments of panic, like all those nightmares when you try to run and can't. And your body, which a second before was muscle and bone and oxygen exploding into energy, is suddenly soup, slow and viscous, when what you need more than anything is angles and speed and sharp points to cut wind resistance. I took the stairs two at a time, half-falling at the bottom, while some instinct to survive sorted the relevant facts. There was a garage behind the house and the back light had been on. I headed for the front door.

"Gotta go," I heard Jenny sign off to her friend. "I think they're home."

A car door slammed shut. My legs wouldn't do what I told them, which seemed so simple: run. The hall stretched on and on, one stride, two, three, I could hear the noise my flight path was leaving, a sonic boom of panic, but I didn't care. Another car door shut. My brain recorded that Jenny hadn't put the chain back. I grabbed for the door knob, yanked on it hard, and dove head first into the outside. I didn't bother to shut it behind me, I just pounded down the brick walk, the scent of Joan's flowers getting sucked into my desperate lungs. I whipped the hat off my head and ran and ran and ran. Would they come chasing after? My luck, Nat was a marathon runner in his spare time. Would the police be circling in a minute or two? Would Joan figure it was me? Run, legs, run! I could feel my female bulk of hips and thighs still resisting the demand to be air, not earth, but I was around the corner now, Steed waiting just ahead, and glancing back no one was following. Yet. I fumbled with my keys, my fingers clumsy with adrenaline. In a moment she was free and together we became, finally, a creature of flight.

I aimed for the smallest, darkest, curviest streets in J. P., thanking some long-dead, half-assed colonial street planners for their condensed and creative design.

It was ten o'clock when I wheeled my weary Steed safely into her sunporch stall, and I only had enough energy for one final thought.

If Chloe Frasier grew up to be a male-identified, lesbian-hating little shit, I was going to be pissed.

TEN

I woke up the next morning feeling strangely refreshed. You'd think by now my attitude would be in serious need of adjusting: a broken heart, a drunk mom, a missing four-year-old being subjected to who knew what. No job, no prospects, and the only skills I was acquiring were not exactly marketable. I wondered how Illegal Entry Specialist would look on my resume. Yeah, but it wasn't even like I had $10,000 in ill-gotten gains to show for it. Well, under job responsibilities I could list impersonation, concealing self, and running for life. I should work it up and take it with me next time Ms. Allen wanted me to bask in the joy of her presence.

But the sun was shining and the sky was perfect blue out my windows and the building was quiet. It was that feeling of stealing time, like I was supposed to be somewhere, registered, accounted for, punched in, named and numbered, with a hall pass and an ID card, but I'd slipped between the bureaucratic cracks, and the day was mine. The life was mine, really. I grinned and let the soft sheets linger on my skin a moment longer. Whatever happened, I'd be okay.

Noon found me at the BPL. That's the Boston Public Library to the uninitiated. This is a great library, and I'm speaking as a connoisseur here. I love libraries. Always have. Something about the quiet keeps me still and that's what I need sometimes. The wealthier suburbs have some good ones, Brookline's being notable because they subscribe to *Off Our Backs,* and when my subscription lapses due to poverty, I can always count on the good citizens of Brookline to keep me in touch with the movement.

But the BPL. Now there's a library. The ceilings are like a hundred feet high and the windows are probably the same square footage as my apartment, and there's these big old wooden tables that have claw feet and books about everything. Everything. And if they don't have it, they'll get it for you on inter-library loan. If you want to see pictures of wild horses, it's there. If you need to find out about Paleolithic burial customs, the BPL won't let you down.

Anyway, it's a good thing I like libraries, since I was there all afternoon, rolling reel after reel of microfiche past my eyes. I started with Saturday and worked my way back. It got so flat so fast: votes cast, car crashes, fashion trends, armies growing like clouds while beneath them puddles of dead and wounded grew and grew. There was a picture of a child with her eyes burned out. I stared and stared. There was a picture of Nelson Mandela being sworn into office. There was a picture of an anorexic woman with mean, spiky hair in a $2,000 bustier. Thanks so much, Madonna. It's easy to blame women, I know, but there's nothing I hate more than people selling out on their own kind. And then thinking it's some kind of fucking act of courage.

After awhile I stopped reacting and just read, disengagingmy heart to try to save it, and then wondering if that's how hearts were killed. Do you lose either way? Meanwhile the words fled by, each one weighed down with meaning, a victory or a loss, another human event in an all too human world. By the end of the first hour, I wanted a cookie, preferably chocolate, which is a grown up way of saying I wanted my mommy. By the end of the second hour, I wanted the greenhouse effect to start ASAP. Run a fever, big blue marble, kill us all in self-defense. It's too far out of whack, this Homo Sapien experiment, and the people who remember how to hold the balance are almost all gone. Bulldozed forests, small pox blankets, women bound and burned and all their knowledge with them.

All this and more, in *The Boston Globe*.

Eventually, I found what I wanted. The date was a year and a half ago and the title was "Brookline Woman Arrested For Drugs." I sat up straighter and felt a little more alive. The police had found $20,000 worth of unnamed drugs in the possession of Diane Frasier. She'd been stopped for a traffic violation and the drugs were in her car. Her bail was set at $25,000. Just the facts,

Ma'am.

But why? Where? How had they found the drugs? I rewound the spool with a little too much force and tried to give myself a pep talk. All right, now you know for a fact that Diane was busted for drugs, and you know the date, so okay, you got that right from the Doctor-Diane interchange, that's good. That's really good. So what's next? I gathered my thoughts for round two of the BPL while the machine printed out a copy for me.

What was next was a pit stop at the reference desk, where the friendliest people in the world live.

"Hi," I said to the woman at the desk. "I need information about a drug. It's a prescription drug and, like, the side effects and stuff like that . . ."

You don't even need to use complete sentences at the library. They know exactly what you mean.

The librarian smiled and nodded and rose from her chair. She was petite, with blunt cut hair gone gray all over, which she didn't dye. I liked her.

"The place to start is *The Physician's Desk Reference*. Right over here," she replied, leading the way.

She showed me how to use it and said if I had any more questions just to ask and we could do more research, and I wanted to leave fruit, flowers and votive offerings at her altar. You know what it is? They never make you feel stupid, librarians, and they never ask why.

It didn't take two minutes for me to discover that fluoxetine hydrochloride was an eight syllable word for Prozac; that Diane's three bottles had contained the recommended dosage; that only nine people had killed themselves with Prozac; and that the drug was also available in a mint-flavored liquid. Mmm. I bet that was yummy.

But what did any of it mean, I wondered as I closed the book. It was after four. Enough Diane for one day. We had a rehearsal tonight and I had to practice. I put the book away and headed home.

ELEVEN

"We've only got ten weeks," Jaye was saying in a serious tone. "It seems like a long time—"

But just then the door flew open and Amy was right behind it.

"I'm here!" she announced, throwing her arms wide. "And I'm ready!"

"Your hair!" me and Katie and Jaye shrieked all at once. It had gone from six inches past her shoulders to half an inch from her scalp.

"I'm not going to Minnesota as a straight girl. It's too humiliating. And let's get real. This has been taking way too long. I'm a lesbian," she sang, and sang again. "Lesbian!"

Then she passed her head around for us to pet and we oohed and aahed at its velvet hand and I think we all felt a little giddy, but serious, too. I wished there was a ceremony, to welcome her to the tribe, some sacred vows for us all to repeat.

I solemnly swear to love each woman as myself, I promise passionate honor, the tenderest touch, she says, bending on one knee.

And do you pledge, we ask her, to defend the women of earth, their lives and their daughters, richer and poorer, in sickness and health?

I do, she replies.

Then by the power invested in all of us, we declare you lesbian, touching a life-sized labrys to each of her shoulders.

For the glory of love and the Goddess! the women shout, as Amy tosses her bouquet to a crowd of uninitiated girls. With a flick from her knife, she's free from the garter that clung to her leg, the last vestige of female submission, and she drops it ceremoniously in a blazing trash can . . .

"I still can't believe we're really going," Katie said.

At this we all took a deep breath. The Minnesota Wimmin's Music Festival. It was the biggest and oldest and we'd sent them a demo tape and they'd liked it. I know we were like the warm-up for the warm-up for the warm-up, but it was officially the night stage. And Minnesota meant one thing. Producers. Contracts. Our shot at the big time. A chance for a break.

"Let's get to it," Jaye said, taking up position behind her drums.

I slipped Ricki's strap over my head, Katie hit the power button on her amp, and Amy started swaying to a beat that hadn't started yet. I love that moment. It's like the end of a long summer evening with someone you're not sure of. You've been circling for hours, her shoulder brushes yours and you can almost smell her skin and now it's night, thick and dark and quiet and are you or aren't you, meanwhile your circles are getting smaller, will it be sweet or wild or will it leave you wanting more and will you get to find out . . .

We played for an hour until everyone started getting cranky, and then Jaye asked if anyone had eaten dinner.

No, of course not.

"Let's order pizza," Katie suggested, "on me."

"I'd offer you guys snacks, but food stamps haven't arrived and the cupboard is bare," I apologized and tried not to feel humiliated.

"I should have brought day-olds from the restaurant," Amy protested.

"I could have picked up something on my way over," Katie said.

"Okay, so we're all a bunch of shits," Jaye quipped, picking up the phone. "Is Pizza Towne okay? They've got whole wheat."

Everyone agreed and I headed for the bathroom. There were still rays of sun coming through the window above the claw-foot tub. The floor had small blue tiles set in perfect rows, their surfaces gone satiny smooth with age. Jaye's soap left a faint smell of apples. I could hear my friends laughing down the hall. I washed my hands and saw my reflection glancing back at me. Short brown hair, big brown eyes, teeth slightly crooked. How I'd hated my teeth when I was twelve, the year I'd realized that some people had money and some people didn't and braces weren't going to happen. The unfairness of it twisting into more self-hate. Surely it had to be my fault. I had stared into the mirror then, as if I could provide an answer for myself, until my mother would holler, "Skyler, what the hell are you doing in there?" and I'd look away in relief.

I leaned closer to the mirror and looked at my teeth, a whole set of rugged individualists, refusing to toe the line, non-conformist little chunks of bone. Crooked. What the hell, they matched my grin.

Still grinning, I headed back down the hall and into a room that was suddenly quiet. I looked from Amy to Katie, who were both staring at me in the strangest way, and then to Jaye, who stood in the kitchen doorway.

"What's going . . ." I started to ask but didn't need to finish. In one hand Jaye was holding a small white bag. The Bagel Bakery, it said in blue, with red bagels scattered randomly across it. In the other hand she held a fistful of little pill-filled plastic bags.

"Skyler?" she asked, utterly confused.

"Shit," I said, feeling the heat hit my face. "You guys, it's not what you think."

"I don't know what I think," Jaye replied, her words like a slow, steady pace.

"They're not mine," I said, trying to reassure them. Katie and Amy were still staring. There was a moment of silence. "Okay, um . . . I guess I better tell you the whole story. Have a seat, everyone."

So I did, starting with Diane Frasier and the Evil Doctor at the bank machine, and continuing on to my near run-in with Fuzzy Wuzzy and Friend at Diane's, the contents of her purse, my triple header at the Strausses', the phone call to April Gordon, and what I'd discovered at the BPL, with all praises due to the reference librarian. They'd started with their eyes big and their mouths small, but their mouths had grown wider and wider during the telling, helped along by gasps of horror from Amy and well-rounded expletives from Katie. I ended with a showing of the actual purse owned by Diane Frasier, with the contents unchanged from the day she died.

"Jesus, Skyler, all this and your mom, too," Jaye said, amazed.

And Judith dumped me, I wanted to say for the sympathy. So I did. And was not disappointed. A gratifying chorus of "Oh, Skyler!" was sent heavenward, and I tried to look stoic, though I found myself wanting to cry.

"But, Skyler," said Amy, leaning back on her hands and stretching out one long, languid leg, "before we get any further with this, I just have to know one thing. Why didn't you tell us? I mean, aren't we your friends, or what?"

"Yeah," Katie added, while Jaye did her self-satisfied smirk. Great, now I was going to have to hear all her ACOA twelve-step codependent issues explanations of my psyche. I just like being alone, okay? I wanted to snap, but I couldn't. Amy was right. They were my friends, and I had forgotten that.

I'd known Jaye almost four years. I'd even met her parents, her mom with a smile too sharp to mean it, big gold earrings and shoes with bows. Middle class tacky through and through. I'd sat between Jaye and her step dad at dinner, and all I could think about was Jaye on the bathroom floor every morning the week before they arrived, vomiting up an empty stomach, like her body was trying to get to the bottom, while her memory threw up nightmares night after night. "Am I going crazy?" she whispered, while she cried, so quiet. "I can't remember."

He was slime, Lance Tanner, his lips pale and pasty, calling to the waitress with "Hey, you," and a flick of his finger. After they left she'd finally remembered. How he'd held her down in the back seat of his big American car and shoved his big American dick into her mouth. She was seven years old, with a little elf hair cut and a blue bathing suit with yellow stars and plastic flip flops. Some vacation.

I'd known Katie almost as long. A dirt poor girl from North Carolina, we all loved how she talked, all sugar and slow. "Say it again," we'd beg, waiting. She'd roll her blue eyes, but she'd smile. She played softball every summer and worked at the battered women's shelter. Katie had a scar on her forehead from a steel-toed boot that had been aimed at her half-conscious mother. You always hear about mother instinct, this semi-biological urge to protect the young, but never the reverse. There's not even a word for it. Child instinct? Daughter right? What do you call it? Love?

And Amy. In some ways we were the closest. Maybe it was that her orphanhood made us similar, or the way her voice went with my bass, or maybe it was the unspoken sex we'd never had, but wanted to. I don't know. She'd hit the streets at fifteen and turned tricks to survive but never talked about it now. If a week went by and I didn't see her, we'd be on the phone for at least an hour, me listening to her deadpan stories with punchlines delivered precision-clean. A musician through and through. And then I'd talk, my stories more absurd, all impressions and exaggeration, drama without a climax, nonsensical details wrapped around some outrage that had no resolution. God, how we laughed.

"You're right," I said. "I don't know. Why didn't I tell you. It's nothing personal."

"On your knees," Amy replied, pointing to the floor. "I wanna hear some of those 'Hail, Mary's' you Catholics are famous for. But let's substitute 'Amy' for 'Mary'."

I dutifully assumed a pious pose and began reciting.

"Hail, Amy, full of grace—"

"Full of grace," Amy interrupted. "I don't know."

"Okay. Hail, Amy, full of shit—

"Hey! Is that any way to talk to your mother?" she demanded, while Katie and Jaye snickered.

"Sorry, Ma, " I said contritely. "Hail, Amy, fair of face—"

"Okay, I can live with that."

"—the Lord is witchy. Blessed art thou among women, and blessed is thy Fruit of the Loom underwear."

"I don't believe this," Katie groaned.

"Holy Amy," I pushed on, "Mother of God—

"No, no," she broke in with an imperious wave, "I'm not that boy's mother."

"Holy Amy," I began again, "Other of God—"

"I'm not sure about that one, either," Jaye interjected.

"Holy Amy," I repeated emphatically, "Killer of God—"

"Now we're getting somewhere," Amy said, lifting her chin and gazing angelically into the distance.

"—pray for our dinners, now and at the hour of our deaths. Awomen."

Amy sighed and smiled beautifically. "You're pardoned."

"Does everybody need one?" I asked.

"No, no, I think I'm all set," Jaye replied.

"I'm fine, thanks," added Katie.

Then the doorbell rang and we all sprang into action. Three minutes later we were feasting on fat, with just enough vegetables sprinkled on top to let us pretend otherwise. Some things taste too good to cause cancer.

"So you've been working the drug angle," Jaye said, relaxing back in her chair. None of the kitchen chairs matched: one green, one blue, and two yellow. But they all had four legs and nice place to lean your back and they were all sturdy, biodegradable and free. I had a momentary flash that they were metaphors for my life: found objects that caused no harm, with that rare kind of beauty that no one noticed, too individual to fit neatly, but somehow it all came together.

"What are the facts here?" Amy added, "about the drugs? From the beginning, Skyler," she warned.

"From the beginning. Okay. Well, the first thing was the doctor at the bank machine. He made this threatening kind of comment like, 'If the police find more cocaine in your car, you'll never see Chloe again.' Then Diane said, 'So that was you.'"

"Sounds to me like they set her up," Katie said, picking a mushroom off her pizza. She's a finicky eater.

"Yeah," agreed Jaye.

"Then there's her purse, which you've all seen. In the medicine cabinet were two unopened bottles of the fluoexy-stuff—the Prozac, and there was also a bottle in her purse. Not in the bag of other drugs, but loose, with her hairbrush and stuff. All three are identical."

"And unopened," Jaye pointed out.

"Yeah, none of them were opened," I agreed.

"How happy does anyone need to be?" Amy said, unsticking a piece of mozzarella from the pizza box and lazily dropping it into her mouth. "Sounds like another set-up."

"Were all the pills from the same place?" Katie asked.

"Yeah, a pharmacy in Wellesley," I replied.

"Oh, right," said Jaye. "She lives in Brookline, works downtown, and drives to Wellesley to get her prescriptions filled."

"Well, exactly. I figured the drug bust was a set-up and so was this. They wanted to make it look like a drug suicide. Also," I remembered suddenly, "the little fascist and his friend we're very pleased that her purse was gone, like that the police had taken it. I mean, I had it, but you know what I mean."

"So what do you think? She wasn't doing drugs, but she was dealing?" Jaye asked.

"Maybe she was, maybe she wasn't, in terms of doing them. But she could have been selling them. Maybe the Strausses were new clients. I don't know."

"And that April Gordon? What did you want with her?" Katie asked.

"It was a shot in the dark. Joan Strauss gave Diane the number, so there's something going on there. I don't know, I figured I would run through my phoney drug survey and just see if I could get her talking."

"Try it from this angle," Jaye said slowly. "The boys are looking for her will. Nathan Strauss is a lawyer."

"With an unmarked folder of articles about her death," I added. "I know Joan was lying to me. I know it."

"A liar from the pit of hell," Katie added in her best fire and brimstone. Preacher voice, she calls it.

"Maybe it's a coincidence, maybe not. But there could be a connection. Wills are legal documents," Jaye finished, looking intently at us all.

"Do you have a proposal for us, Jaye?" Amy asked,

draping an arm across Jaye's shoulder.

Jaye grinned. "No, I think that's Skyler's department."

"You want to break into his office?" I asked, trying not to giggle. This couldn't be real.

"Hey, I'm not putting any ideas into anyone's head," Jaye answered, holding up both hands in a universal gesture of innocence and goodwill. No one was fooled.

"How could we get in?" Amy asked to the room in general.

"There's always drain pipes and fire escapes. Maybe we could find an unlocked window," Katie said.

The rest of us blinked uncomprehendingly.

"You're kidding," Jaye replied, voicing our collective chicken-shittedness.

"No, I am not kidding, sugar. I can shinny up a hickory tree faster than a rat snake, why not a drain pipe?"

Three pairs of eyes narrowed, making the same calculations. Katie probably weighed ninety pounds dripping wet. Why not indeed?

"But what if you can't let the rest of us in without a key?" Amy asked petulantly.

"Well, then ya'll just have to trust me, won't you?" came Katie's reply.

TWELVE

As it turned out, we needed Katie's skills and we didn't need a key. Luckily, lawyers are the kind of people who tend to be listed in the phone book. Nathan's office was on a small, narrow street near the State House, which is a very redundant way of saying that the old parts of Boston were built to be up close and personal. The building was brick, but then so was everything in a mile radius, including the sidewalks. There were lamp posts painted black and little details everywhere in wrought iron and brass and dark ivy moving gracefully upwards. All we needed was fog rolling in from the harbor to make the scene complete.

The front of the building was secured by iron bars across the lower windows and lots of foot traffic. Without having to discuss it, we headed down the nearest side street, making a right at the first alley. Soon we were staring at the back of the building, which, like all the others, had a small courtyard enclosed by a large brick wall.

"Now what?" Jaye asked softly.

Amy and I were giggling too hard to reply. Trying to suppress it only made it worse until I felt like the pressure was going to press my gray matter out my nose. The image of brain being extruded like play-doh left my sides aching from silent laughter.

"The two giggle queens give me a leg up," whispered Katie, taking charge. "Time to put those seventy inches to work. C'mon, take a deep breath, that's right."

We both did as told a few times. As long as I didn't look Amy in the eye, we might stay calm.

"Jaye, you keep a watch out," Katie instructed. "Now, you two, move up against the wall. Bend down and let me step in your hands."

"Katie, that wall must be ten feet high. You'll never reach," Amy insisted.

"I'm not done telling you what's what. After you're all straight—"

"—Upright," I corrected.

"Yes, thank you, Skyler. After you've resumed the

correct vertical posture of strong, young lesbians, then I will commence to step from your hands onto your shoulders."

"What?" Amy asked, finally looking up and blinking slowly for emphasis. "You're going to what?"

"I'm going to stand on your shoulders," Katie repeated matter-of-factly.

"Katie," asked Amy in an ominous tone, "have you done this before?"

"I think you need to rephrase that," I whispered back, mimicking her tone. "Katie, have you health insurance?"

"And just what do you people do for childhoods up here?"

We both shrugged. "Try to ride the subway for free?" I offered.

"Barbarians," Katie snorted, pushing us both toward the wall. We cupped our hands as told and Katie mounted up like they were stirrups.

"Going up," I whispered, and Amy started giggling again. Katie whacked her in the side of the head. Then she leaned both hands on the wall for balance as we stood up. I could see she was still a good two feet from the top.

"Red alert," Jaye whispered suddenly. "Somebody's coming—don't move." She stepped back against the wall beside me. At the mouth of the alley a group of teenagers were making their presence known, laughing in this wired-up macho way that was covered with a light coat of boredom. I held perfectly still, breathing in the dusty smell of brick, and tried not to think about how heavy Katie was getting. They didn't notice us, but I didn't like the noise.

"All clear," Jaye said when they'd passed, resuming her post.

Katie's foot left my hands and found my shoulder. I held it firmly in place, which was obviously more for emotional reassurance, but that goes a long way in these situations. For a second I felt the her full weight as she transferred her other foot to Amy's shoulder. It probably wouldn't have hurt so bad if she'd been barefoot, but I lived through it. One of those Bionic Man moments.

And then there we were, perfectly balanced like the proverbial three-legged table that never wobbles, done in vertical. It was stunning really. Then the weight was gone and I was watching Katie's little butt disappear over the wall. We all heard the small thud as she hit the ground, and then some vague rustling as she made her way over to the door in the wall.

Ten seconds later, we were all inside the courtyard.

"There's no lock," she said, ushering us inside, "just a big old deadbolt. C'mon."

"If my mother could see me now," Jaye whispered to no one in particular. It was still a game, but it was becoming a serious one.

"Listen, everybody," I said, stopping them all. I took a long drag of warm spring air and noticed suddenly what a nice courtyard it was. There were small ferns and a miniature tree and little shrubs with peach and white flowers. Brick steps wound round a birdbath and there was a set of chairs by the tree. I wondered if Joan had designed it all.

"Listen," I repeated and looked at them one by one. "What we're doing constitutes breaking and entering. I don't know if it's a felony, but it's only getting to get worse." I paused here and looked significantly at the building. "What I mean is, you don't have to do this with me. There's no dishonor in deciding not to. The last thing any of us needs is a criminal record. Like it's not hard enough finding a job. I mean, you could even just wait for me in the alley."

"No. Way." Amy said each word was its own sentence.

"I'm with you," Jaye replied.

"I wouldn't miss this for nothing," Katie smiled.

"Are you sure?" I insisted. "I don't know for a fact that the kid's in danger."

"I do," replied Jaye. "The whole story's rotten."

The other two nodded in agreement.

"Okay. Let's try the windows."

There was a door and two windows, all sans bars. We quickly discovered that the door was locked and the windows were just out of reach, so Katie was pressed into service again. Standing in our hands she had plenty of height.

"Don't forget your gloves before you touch anything," Jaye remembered just in time. We'd scrounged up various combinations of winter woollies and dish rubbers before leaving the house.

"Thanks," she whispered back. I could feel her fumbling as she put them on. "It looks like it's not locked but there's a screen in the way," she whispered down to us.

"Break it," Amy directed ruthlessly. I felt the giggles starting again and held my breath so Amy wouldn't catch on. The sound of aluminum being forced out of shape fled down the alley with alarming speed. Katie wobbled for a second, Jaye grabbed her legs to steady her and then next thing I knew something was falling on my head. I'm proud to report that my instinct was to protect Katie. I didn't let go of her with the impulse to duck and cover, I just hunched my shoulders instead. It was okay. It was just the screen, so it didn't really hurt. It clattered to the ground with a very distinct, very loud noise.

"I am so sorry," Katie pleaded, and when somebody with her accent says it, you have to believe them.

"It's okay," I said stoically. "No permanent damage. Can you get in?"

"Lift me up a couple of inches," she said, and we tried to oblige. Jaye put her back into it, too, and while it didn't have the grace of the wall scaling, it was effective. In she went, head first, and in thirty seconds we heard her unlocking the door.

"Welcome to Tara," Amy whispered in her best cheesy melodrama voice, which even made Jaye giggle.

"Okay," I said at the threshold, "are you guys sure?"

"It's all for one and one for all," Amy said, like the concept might be difficult but if I stretched my tiny, little brain I could get it. She shouldered past me and into the building.

"Yeah," Jaye muttered, right behind her.

I brought up the rear and we were in. We stood quietly for a minute, getting used to still less light, hearing each other breathe. The building had that smell of professional places, some mixture of slightly new carpet, Xerox ink, wool suits and coffee. I could see straight down the hall to the front door. Rooms opened up off either side, starting with a kitchen to my left and a bathroom to my right.

"Anybody gotta go?" I whispered, and everyone burst into giggles.

"Let's split this up and make it quick," said Jaye, ever the organizer. "I'll take this floor, Amy take the second, Katie take the top, and Skyler, you find Nathan's office and take that."

"What are we looking for?" Amy asked as we started down the hall.

"Anything about Diane Frasier, I guess," I shrugged and started to wonder if the whole idea wasn't a little half-baked. What we were we expecting: a To Do Today pad with "Pick up illegal drugs from Diane" written on it?

We passed a conference room with a large wooden table and tasteful Art-with-a-capital-"A" on the walls, and then Jaye veered off into the reception area by the front door. And then there were three . . .

We tiptoed up the stairs which had that ubiquitous rich people white carpet, just like the hall. Personally, I just don't get it. Especially considering that there were probably gorgeous hardwoods crying for recognition there beneath DuPont's finest, and which would look great no matter how many cups of coffee got spilled on them. I was distracting myself, I knew, but it was hard to focus too much on the here and now without my knees starting to shake.

The door at the top of the stairs was half ajar. There was a tasteful brass plaque that said "Michael Nelson." The room was obviously the secretary's domain. Mikey's actual office must be the room next to it, opening off the secretary's by an interior door.

"This is where I must leave you," Amy said with a sigh, looking over her shoulder as she wandered, wraith-like, through the open door like some kind of Victorian heroine.

"Where'd they make her?" Katie murmured, not expecting an answer.

The same white carpet covered the hall and I could see that it had gained the next flight of stairs as well. The Carpet That Ate Boston. These people just didn't give up, did they? What, there wasn't enough snow for them, they had to cover their floors with white fluffy stuff? It must be a control thing, so they could feel like they'd conquered even the little bits of earth that came in on people's shoes.

There was another suite of rooms at the end of that floor, only this time the little brass plaque said "Nathan Strauss."

"I guess this is my exit," I nodded to Katie. "Good luck."

The door was open and I slipped in without touching it. I put my gloves on, a pair of turquoise and pink ones handmade by someone in Guatemala, in our possession courtesy of Jaye's mom. Hey, we knew they'd come in handy eventually.

There was more light here than in the hall, spilling in from the street. The set-up seemed identical to Mike's, with the secretary acting as a buffer zone for the Big Man in the office behind. The secretary's desk was in the middle of the room, done in basic black steel. I guess they call them "Work Stations" now because of the computer and all. It was intensely efficient, not a paper clip out of place and not a coffee cup in sight. A large desk calendar was opened crisply to the correct page—namely, tomorrow. Goddess, these people were too much. I had myself a seat and read back over the last few weeks. There was nothing about Diane and nothing listed on any of the weekends, including last Saturday. Oh well.

I got up and went to the row of file cabinets against the wall. Each drawer was clearly marked as to its alphabetically correct contents, so it wasn't hard to find the F's. It only took a minute to come up with nothing. Oh well again.

Down the hall there was a sudden loud clatter of something hitting the floor. I jumped like I'd gotten a shock.

"Oh, fuck," Amy stage-whispered in mock terror. I didn't bother to ask if she was okay. I headed toward Nathan's room, one hand over my hammering heart, pledging allegiance to my own safety. There was sweat gathering on my forehead, which must have been where all the moisture in my throat had gone. I tried swallowing again and looked around. It was all steel and glass, that kind of modern, masculine stuff that anyone under the age of five would mangle themselves on, all angles and edges and punishing corners. And that same goddamn white carpet.

I took up residence behind his desk and began sorting through his neat stacks of papers. For a few minutes hopelessness overcame terror as my primary emotion. None of this was any use: files filled with notes on people I would never meet and couldn't care less about. One divorce, two, a prenuptial agreement, and another divorce. I wondered if he ever worried that it might infect him, like how cancer surgeons get cancer way more often then the average. I settled back in the chair and laced my fingers behind my head. The gesture made me want to put my feet up on the desk. Or better yet, leave a footprint right smack in the middle of it.

Jesus, Gabriel, you're in the middle of a fucking felony. Keep it together already.

I reached down and started going through his drawers. Legal pads, expensive-looking pens, an electric razor and a small mirror, and a box of condoms. Eeeew, gross. Just what did this guy do on his lunch break?

In the bottom I found a picture frame—the kind that sit up on your desk—facing down. I lifted it out and turned it over. There was a man with his arm around Joan, who smiled up at me, her hair short and tousled. They were sitting on a porch swing holding an infant. An infant with white skin. An infant not Lisa.

I got up and took the picture to the window for a better look. No way was this the child I'd seen at the Strausses'. I assumed the man was Nathan, but who was the kid? Maybe it was a niece, or a friend of the family. Yeah, maybe. Or maybe not. I turned the frame over and undid the latches, slipping the back off. For once in this world, something's actually convenient. The month and year were stamped in neat blue rows across the back of the photo. It was almost four years old.

I thought hard while I reassembled the frame and put it back where I'd found it. Maybe they'd had this kid first, but then Joan couldn't have more. That letter I'd read from her friend with cancer, there'd been a definite implication of illness or trauma or loss. If they'd had a baby, and couldn't have more, and then the child died, well, that'd be enough grief for one lifetime. It could explain why they'd adopted—and if the guy in the photo was Nathan, then Lisa was adopted, because he was definitely white. Though people adopt for lots of reasons. It would also explain why this photograph, framed and obviously meant for display—was face down in the bottom drawer. But did it have anything to do with Diane Frasier?

It felt like time to leave. I heard Katie's light steps on the stairs. She must have thought so, too. I met her in the hall and we wordlessly went to collect Amy.

She was sitting on the floor picking through a small trash basket and even in the dark I could see her resigned martyr expression.

"Let's go," I whispered.

She perked up immediately, lifting the basket between two fingers and placing it back beside the secretary's desk.

"Any luck?" I asked.

"Nah," she shrugged. "You?"

"I don't think so, but I'll tell you about it later."

We tiptoed down the stairs in a quiet line. I could feel the sweat collecting every place where skin met skin. I was gonna be glad when this was over.

"Jaye," Katie whispered, leaning from the waist into the reception area. It was dead quiet.

"Jaye," Amy chimed in.

"Okay, one, two, three," I gave the count.

"Jaye," we whispered in unison.

"I'm coming, I'm coming," she replied, appearing from a dark doorway off to the left. She had something in her hand.

"Look what I found," she said in an ominous tone.

It was a manila folder. She tapped the little tab where the name goes. In the dim light I could just barely read the two typed words: Frasier, Diane.

"Goddamn," I said under my breath.

"Empty," said Jaye, letting it fall open for emphasis.

"Where'd you find it?" I asked.

"There's a copy room next door. They've got a nice Xerox machine, and guess what else?" She relaxed into the pause.

"A paper shredder."

"No," gasped Amy.

"Yeah. But there's a box beside it where I guess they put folders that can be re-used. This was right on top."

"Goddamn," I said again. We all stared at the folder for a minute.

"Guess we better wrap this up," I said, taking charge.

The front door was dead-bolted and inoperable without a key. Katie said the screen was too busted to try to put back. We decided we'd just have to just walk out the back and through the garden. Nobody could think of a way for Katie to get back over the wall by herself, so we'd just have to leave the garden door unlocked.

"Maybe they'll think one of them left it open and then someone broke the screen trying to get in," I said.

Jaye went to put the folder back and the rest of us started down the hall. We waited at the threshold for Jaye to catch up. I listened to Amy's breathing, taking comfort in the soft, steady sound, I realized that without even saying it we'd all agreed: no one leaves until we're all leaving. The loyalty was assumed, and here in the dark, in a building we'd gained illegal entry to, my stomach like a steel girder through my mid-section, I saw how much I assumed in them. That we'd stick together; that the law held no moral authority; that the safety of a little girl mattered, and enough to do what we were doing. No one asked me why: why I had tried, why I had cared. In a world where female lives had mattered so little, an almost abstract Chloe Frasier was something we would fight for. For a moment, I had no fear, too stunned at the open wonder of my heart. I had friends and love was possible.

"Let's go," said Jaye, bringing up the rear.

We moved in a line, a solemn procession now, all the wildness left behind. I heard Jaye pull the door shut as I led the way back to the garden door. The moon sat swollen in the sky and even through the city lights she reached us. It was so quiet here, the small noise of us lost in the huge night sky. I wanted stars, all the ones the street lights held back, all the ones I'd never seen, their light a million years old, their burning bodies long since dead and buried in this sea of night which was just another kind of earth, I wanted more and more and more.

I opened the door and the alley was empty of human beings except for their evidence. Refuse and bottles and broken cardboard and still I wanted more, the slicing edge of glass that started as sand and glimmered now, precious as gold. I could smash it beneath my heel and sprinkle the pieces in Amy's virgin hair, make a circle for Katie's wrist, set a curve against Jaye's throat. Food wrappers glowed white, crinkling like gauze, we could make a train to trail behind us, the Queens of This Place, the Alley Behind, the Land of Locked Garden Doors. Stand in attendance while we pass, we who see beauty, it's all just tricks of light and the application of the heart or what's left of it. Rip it out, what you find inside, and throw it high, as high as you can, and maybe the stars will catch it or maybe it will fall here, in an alley, ruby red pieces for a vagabond priestess and her wandering queens.

I watched as Jaye shut the door and then we looked from one to the other, our eyes dark and colorless, until Amy said, "Let's get the fuck out of here," and whatever it was, it was over. I wanted to take them all by the hand and run, our language physical as wild dogs turning wolves, I wanted to make them swear they'd remember, no, I wanted to not have to ask, remembering like a movement, you couldn't lose a verb.

Katie's eyes were blue now, I could see. We

rounded the corner and Jaye's were brown and the nape of Amy's neck was naked and clean.

And there was a cop up ahead, walking toward us.

"Everybody have fun," I chatted amiably.

"So whose car should we take to Minnesota?" Jaye said conversationally.

"I guess we should take Evie. I'm just nervous for her," Amy answered, her drawl only slightly off, or maybe it was my ears going funny with the rising tension. Had somebody seen us or heard us and were we about to spend the night in a cement block hotel at the tax-payers expense? My heart felt swollen from its reckless pounding, stretching to pump faster and faster. If it burst would I drown? He was ten feet away, and the distance was shrinking fast. Oh God, let this be over. I watched him look us up and down.

"Does she need any new parts? We could all chip in," I heard myself speaking like a voice on the phone, long distance, from Paris or Nairobi or Katmandu, someplace you've never been and can only barely imagine. It sounded high and thin and a little too fast.

"Well, at least an oil change. I'll see what else the mechanic suggests," Amy replied evenly. He was almost on top of us. I could actually see the whites of his eyes.

"Let us know," Jaye said, very sincerely.

"Good evening, boys," said Mr. Policeman, with just enough threat to let us know we were being put in our place.

Good evening, Officer, I wanted to reply in a saccharine, school-room singsong.

"Good evening," said Jaye, perfectly calm.

He kept his eyes on us but he also kept going.

Until Amy had to add, "You know, we're not boys. We're lesbians."

So then he had to stop, his eyes narrowing as he looked us over more closely. I realized that Amy and him had the same haircut.

"Oh," he said, his awkwardness making a quick translation into more arrogance. "Excuse me. Good evening, ladies." His 'ladies' was hands-down the ugliest word.

"No problem. You too," said Amy in a very slow drawl over her shoulder, as we were already past him. I gave her a non-verbal elbow nudge, which can be translated loosely to mean: would you quit while you're ahead and shut the fuck up?

"I can't believe you did that," said Jaye, in an ultra-pleasant tone as we rounded the corner. The car was in sight. Please, God, just get us home.

"I can't either," she said expressionlessly. Truth be told, she looked a little stunned. "That was the first time I ever—well . . . came out. In public. To a stranger."

We all looked at her with renewed respect.

"To a cop," added Jaye.

"After your first felony," I put in.

Amy sat in the back and looked self-satisfied the whole way home.

THIRTEEN

I'd never been to a funeral parlor before. Actually, I'd never been to a funeral. I realized how strange that was, as if someone could live twenty-four years without death touching them. My surroundings seemed perfect for my musings. The landscaping was so neat and tidy I could've believed it was fake. The building was a giant Victorian house that had been humiliated with aluminum siding and those vinyl frame replacement windows that practically scream "A Petroleum Product Was Here."

People in small groups of two's and three's were heading toward the entrance, their somber colors indicating our common purpose. I looked down at my own clothes: the Basic Interview Outfit, with a plain white shirt. Black trousers, nice black shoes, which I'd bought literally the paycheck before I got my pink slip. And boy was I glad in the long run. Nothing like unemployment to make you need nice clothes, and doesn't that suck. I usually wore a purple silk shirt with it, a tag sale special with a small coffee stain that was completely concealed by my black linen jacket. But Jaye's white blouse was more apropos to the circumstances. All in all I didn't look bad for a working class kid.

Two official-looking white guys in identical black suits hovered at the door, wearing generic expressions of sympathy. I didn't believe it for a minute, but then I don't know if you're supposed to. Inside, the hallway was filled with people and the sound of their subdued chatter. It was strange, like a big party except no one was smiling. I felt conspicuous even though I knew I was blending in fine, and wished one of my friends was with me. Fact finding, not socializing, Gabriel, you're here to get information, not make friends and influence people. There was a big room off to the right, the "chapel" or whatever they call it, with rows of chairs and almost-Muzak organ music playing. I made a mental note to put a "no organ music" clause in my will, if I ever wrote one. Not like I had copious amounts of either possessions or heirs to fight over them, but the awful music was reason enough to write one.

I was starting to get that too-many-hands-and-not-enough-places-to-put-them feeling. Circulate, I commanded, and in a word, eavesdrop.

I moved slowly and without clear intention in a rough circle through the crowd. I'd never realized how hard it was to hear someone when you weren't looking at them, especially in a crowded room.

"It's the little girl I feel sorry for. First Jonathan and now . . ." a woman in a navy silk suit to a man in tasteful pinstripes. There wasn't any way to hear more without obviously stopping to listen.

". . . donations, but I sent flowers, too. It just didn't seem . . ."

". . . her best work. It really made me open to the emotional . . ."

I was just starting to get frustrated with the funeral chit chat when I saw him. The Bad Man. The Doctor. I felt my heart thump its way upward into my throat. Calm, stay calm. He's never seen you, and there's no reason for him to notice you now. I kept my eyes lowered to the dark red carpet, as I ambled discreetly toward him. He was standing by the door to the chapel in a very expensive suit, his blond hair perfect and short, intensely handsome in this way that was totally repulsive. He was well over six feet tall and he knew it, all hard muscle and almost military tension. All except the eyes. There was something bored in his eyes, the way his lids closed, slowly, when you'd expect it to be fast. I had an almost visceral impression of his sexual behavior and it wasn't pretty.

A woman approached him and they started talking. I could hear their voices but not their words. She was short and plump with comfortable shoes, bright lipstick, and brown skin. Her hair was cut up close to her scalp and I liked the way her eyes looked alive. She was wearing a red suit but it didn't seem out of place because she was the type that anything dull would have looked strange on.

I had reached the opposite side of the doorway, so I stopped and began looking through the crowd as if I'd lost someone and was trying to locate them.

"What she needs is some stability," my woman in red was saying, putting a hand firmly on her hip.

"I appreciate your concern and we'll—"

I lost the next few lines as a het couple passed slowly through the doorway. I had this terrible urge to say, I know you're grief stricken and all, but could you put a move on it?, while giving them a pleasant shove from behind. It was intensely frustrating.

"Listen, Dr. Gunther—"

Dr. Gunther, Dr. Gunther, Dr. Gunther. I smiled and waved at no one in particular. I had his name, I could conquer the world.

"I don't mean any offense, but I don't think you know anything about children. I don't think you appreciate at all what that child's going through."

Her hackles were up and I couldn't blame her. His words were polite but he was full of shit. Meanwhile the lights dimmed discreetly and people started moving toward the door. God fucking damn it.

"Mrs. Jarmon, my wife and I will discuss your concerns. Now if you'll excuse me, the service is starting," he said in a cool, professional, and generally dismissive tone, and smiled. Ick. Then he turned and walked right by me into the chapel.

"Mmm," she snorted, shaking her head. I tried to catch her eye and she was happy to oblige.

"Some people," she said, shaking her head some more.

I smiled in agreement. She turned and headed into the chapel and I stepped in beside her.

"Were you a friend of Diane's?" I asked conversationally.

"I'm one of Chloe's teachers," she answered. Up near the front a woman was waving at her. There was exactly one seat saved. So much for that lead. She headed for her friend and I headed for the back.

I took a seat as close to the aisle as I could get. As the rest of the crowd filtered in, I tried to listen to the people around me, but everyone was speaking in tones respectfully hushed. I sighed and looked around. The woman in front of me had dark red hair that she'd braided and piled on her head, her skin that pale, pale white that bruises in the sun. I always think people like that must be so fragile, delicate like birds, not quite of this world. Did the man beside her take good care? The back of her neck looked soft with tiny hair, and I suddenly wanted to touch her with such terrible sweetness. A man was talking from the podium, delivering generic pieties and Diane deserved better, I wanted to insist, we all did, in our sorrow. The woman bent her head, a Dolor Mater in perfect white. My tenderness felt like grief and maybe it was. The ache in my throat could only be tears, for Diane, for my mother, for Judith, for my own exiled heart. It's an all or nothing deal, I realized as a single tear fell off the precipice of my world eye. All or nothing, these human hearts. You can't take the joy without the pain, and I had to decide. All around I could hear the small sounds of grief, and this is what it meant to love. I had to accept it without retreat: it wasn't like a risk you could run, it was part of the plan, the part that hurt. I closed my eyes and knew there was peace here, if I could only find it.

When the service was over, the people in the aisle waited patiently for the front rows to empty. A glimpse was the only further contact I had with the Doctor. On his arm was a much younger woman draped in dark silk. No one seemed the least bit interested in talking, and how do you make small talk under those circumstances? I waited with everyone else, and thought how loss was the naked bones of love. If there was a wake, I wasn't invited. When it was my turn I filed out into the cool spring air.

FOURTEEN

"You better call me," Amy had warned the night before. So after changing into my usual schleppy dyke jeans, I called her house and left a cryptic message. She does have roommates, after all.

"Hey, Aims, it's Skyler. I got the name of the doctor but nothing else. Gimme a call if you need more. Bye."

Katie got the same, and I tried Jaye at work but she was "in a meeting" so she'd just have to suffer the suspense. In the meantime, I had research to do.

I grabbed the phone books, white and yellow, pulled the phone into my room, and flopped onto the bed. Gunther, "G". I found the right page and a list of some fourteen Gunthers. None of them had those handy little initials, "M. D.", but it was still worth a try. I picked up the phone, rolled onto my stomach, and dialed. Nobody answered, which was probably just as well since I didn't really have a script yet. I hung up and thought hard for a minute.

Flowers. Somebody had placed an order to send flowers but the computer had gotten its little wires crossed and eaten the address. All that was left was the name: Dr. Gunther. So if this was Dr. Gunther's address, we'd send them out ASAP.

What if he asked who was sending the flowers? I'd make up a name. Or maybe I wouldn't give a name, just interrupt with a "Thank you" and hang up. At that point it wouldn't matter. The addresses were all in the phone book.

Feeling fortified, I picked up the receiver and dialed the next Gunther. And the next. Gunthers #1-4 were apparently all gainfully employed. It was starting to get depressing when Gunther #5 answered. Gunther, G. L., I had time to read when a woman's voice answered.

"Hello?"

"Ah, yes, I'm calling from Speedwell Florists and I'm trying to get in touch with a Doctor Gunther. Is this the right number?"

"No, no," replied the voice, slightly annoyed, but

basically friendly. "We've gotten calls for him before. His number's not listed. I don't know why, if I was a doctor I'd sure as hell be listed. I suppose he puts his time in at the office and then he wants everyone to leave him alone. But I'll tell you, it's a pain in the pants for the rest of us Gunthers. His patients can't find his number and call us in the middle of the night. And I have to say, Honey, I can't help you with your troubles and if you want to help me with mine, please do not go through the phone book calling people you don't know at two o'clock in the morning. Am I making myself clear?"

I didn't know if this last was part of her well-worn monologue or pointed at me in particular so I just kinda mumbled, "Ah, yeah."

"But do me a favor. If you figure out his phone number, would you call me back and give it to me? Because I'd like to talk to him about this. And I'd also be very happy to give it out next time someone calls in the middle of the night. At least then I wouldn't be the only one losing sleep." She laughed here, as if on cue, a short, mirthless sound as automatic as a smoker's cough. I wondered how many times she'd delivered this speech.

"Sure, sure. I'm sorry to disturb you. Thanks anyway," I said, and put the receiver down quickly.

So, the guy was unlisted. It was helpful to learn the facts early on, even if the facts themselves weren't helpful, know what I mean? I shoved the white pages to the other side of the bed and opened the yellows. I kid you not, there were over forty pages of physicians. But under their appropriate specialty they were all alphabetically arranged, so that made life a little easier. It only took about three minutes to find him: Gunther, William T. Under Gyn/Ob. Nice. I've heard they're the worst woman-haters of the lot, gynecologists, like they score highest on those "How Much Do YOU Hate Women Tests?"

I picked up the receiver and dialed, hoping the adrenaline would inspire me to new heights of creativity.

"Reproductive Health," said a female voice. The term that best described it was "well-modulated." That tone gives you very little to go on, which I suppose is the point.

"Yes, I need to talk to Dr. Gunther," I said, trying to sound intense and serious. A matter of life and death. Something's gone terribly wrong and only Dr. Gunther can petition the Fates for me.

There was a light pause.

"Dr. Gunther," came the reply, short and strained, "no longer works here."

"But how—I mean—" playing the emotions to the hilt, even though I hadn't filled in the plot yet. My breath shuddered all on its own, a perfect touch.

"I need to talk to Dr. Gunther. Please," I begged, my voice almost cracking, "do you have a new number for him?"

"I'm sorry, that's not information I can give out," came the reply. She was trying to sound mechanical but there was a definite uncertainty.

"You have to let me talk to somebody," I wailed, letting the floodgates of hysteria open wider. "Somebody!"

"Ma'am," she said, trying to gain control, "were you a patient of his?"

"Was I a patient of his?" I returned in utter outrage.

"Okay, all right, Ma'am, I'm going to put you through to someone who can help you, all right?" She must have hit the button lickety-split as instantaneously there was the dead sound of "hold". Ten seconds later a male voice came on.

"This is Dr. Brant. How can I help you?" The tone was very fatherly but underneath I could hear some wariness.

"I need," I said very slowly and intensely, "to talk to Dr. Gunther."

"And what's your name?"

"Oh, no. I'm not giving you my name," I replied wildly. Probably his worst nightmare. A paranoid hypochondriac just oozing some kind of female trouble and on the verge of hysteria.

"Okay, all right, fair enough," he said, giving in immediately. "But if you could give me some idea of the nature of the problem, I might be able to help you."

Here I was stumped. Being a lesbian, I had managed to avoid the cause of most visits to the ob/gyn unit, i.e., heterosexuality and its attendant diseases and cell multiplication. I had no idea what the nature of the problem might be.

"I just need to talk to Dr. Gunther," I said in the slow, flat monotone of a woman on the edge. My toes were wiggling. This was fun.

"Maybe you'd like to come in for an appointment. What we deal with here is often of a personal nature, and maybe you'd feel more comfortable in person."

"I don't think so," I said in a and-you-know-as-well-as-I-do-why kind of tone.

"Did your treatments result in live birth?" he asked conversationally.

There was silence while I tried to figure out my answer, like computing chess moves. If I said "yes", did that narrow down the pool of possible patients, thus rendering "no" the best answer? Were live births more common than . . . what? No births? Dead births? It seemed so sad suddenly, so alien and desperate and arrogant, men playing God as usual over the wide open bodies of women. But I couldn't think about that now. I went on the offensive instead.

"If you don't give me a way to get in touch with my doctor, I'm going to sue your butts off, do you understand?"

"Look," he said slowly. I could practically smell his sweat. "Who else have you talked to about this?"

"Well, my husband, of course," I replied belligerently.

"I think the best thing to do in this situation is for you to come in and speak to someone. If there's medical assistance that you or your child needs, of course we'll provide that. We'll do anything you want."

"What I really want is Dr. Gunther's phone number," I said in that same flat monotone I'd used with the receptionist.

"He's not going to be able to help you," he was pleading with me now. Oh, the humiliation of a rich, white man used to wielding a scalpel.

I tried a little reverse psychology. First, I sighed heavily. Then, in a teary voice, I said, "Please, let me just talk to him. I know you're probably right, and I'll make an appointment to come in. But I just need to talk to him."

"Okay," he said in what was probably his best bedside manner and boy was that a grim thought. "All right. If you hold for just a minute, I'll get it for you."

The phone went blank and I waited. What was the leverage I was pretending to have? Was there something hush-hush going on? I realized I was going to need a pen when he came back. My eyes gave the room a once-over but there wasn't a writing implement in sight. I put the receiver down, ran into the hall, grabbed a handful of pens and pencils, and bolted back into my room.

"Hello? Hello?" I could hear his voice, all thin and tiny, from where the phone lay. I picked it up.

"Yes, I'm here," I said in a long-suffering voice. "I went to get a pen."

He read the number twice to make sure I got it right and it was all I could do not to give a victory hoot.

"Do you have that, Mrs. . . . ?" He was still fishing for my name.

I ignored him. "Thank you, Dr. Brant," I said in a very final tone and began to hang up.

"Wait!" I heard his microscopic plea just before the receiver hit the button and disconnected him.

A quick flip through the telephone directory told me his exchange was in Wellesley which made something go click in my brain. I jumped up and pulled Diane's purse out from under my bed. The pill bottles, all three of them, had been prescribed by one Dr. Gunther and issued by the Bidden Family Pharmacy in guess where.

So now what. Three phone calls seemed in order. The first was to Gunther #5. I figured she deserved it.

"Hello, this is Angela from Speedwell Florists. I have that phone number you were looking for, the Dr. William Gunther who's unlisted?"

She fairly cackled with delight.

The second call was to the BPL. Did I mention

they're just as helpful at a distance? I asked for the reference desk.

"Hi, um, I need to know the name of the company that puts out those reverse telephone directories?" The only reason I know about those is because I'm a Kinsey Milhone fan. I know she's not a real person, but I think she's really cool. Also, she lives in California where it's always warm. This means a lot when you live in Boston. Of course, I'm dying to know what Sue Grafton's gonna do when she gets to those difficult letters, like x and z. X is for Xerox? Z is for zebra? Doesn't exactly have a ring to it.

"Oh, yes, we have those," she replied. She gave me the name of the company and their number.

So that was phone call number three.

"Hi, listen. If my phone number is unlisted in the regular directory, would it be in your reverse directory?"

"Well, it shouldn't be," the woman replied in mild alarm. "Give me your number and I'll check for you."

"No, no, it's not, I mean, ah . . . I'm writing a mystery novel and I needed to know for the plot. But thanks."

So I had his number, but not his address. What next. I glanced up at the clock. I had to go. But I'd keep thinking about it. Maybe I'd have a brilliant inspiration.

FIFTEEN

It was that Wednesday of the month when the revolution called. There's a Boston area feminist newspaper I work on, *The Women's Page*. It comes out once a month. I don't usually write for it, that's not my forté. I like the production end, the typesetting and layout part, making it all fit to the sixteenth of an inch. Since I do the grunt work, I get to pick the typefaces, graphics and border, and it's more fun than you can imagine. I don't know why it gives me such a kick, but it does. Tonight there was an editorial meeting, which meant the mock-ups had to be ready. No sweat, I had the rest of the afternoon.

The office is a two room, third story deal in Central Square. There's three big windows along the back wall, overlooking a crowded parking lot and a crowded row of sad, sagging Victorians. I'd taken over half this wall, claiming I needed the natural light. It wasn't technically true, but nobody seemed to have a preference except me.

I flipped on the light, locked the door from the inside, and saw the huge pile of mail waiting to be opened. Damn. Everyone always waits until the last minute to send in their announcements for dances and housemates. Obviously, no one else from the collective had been in for a few days. Well, I'd try to get to it, but mock-ups came first, so we could have something to agree on at the meeting. I turned on the computer, a vintage Mac that we should be able to donate to the Smithsonian. Somebody's parents had had no further use for it. As long as it made columns, I wasn't going to complain. At this point in the collective's history, nobody could even say for sure who the woman or her parents had been, so quick was the turnover. Alison Chesley, Chelsey West, Lesley Alice and Alison Bechdel ("No, that's the cartoonist," I'd pointed out) were all names that had been offered up to me by umpteenth-generation collective members when I'd wanted someone to psychically thank. Nobody really knew. It kinda scared me, the truncated memory of my political movement.

I commandeered the one comfortable chair in the

place. It swiveled, rolled, leant backward, and was cushioned. Can't ask for more. I pulled a fruit-sweetened, carcinogen-free cola from the shelf above me, popped the can, and settled down to work.

Let's see. There was an interview with a group of welfare moms who'd taken over a row of abandoned houses in Roxbury. The article was great—probably lead story stuff, but we'd need a graphic for the cover since we didn't have a photo. Then there was a book review of Catharine MacKinnon's latest, except the reviewer spelled "MacKinnon" without the little "a". Go figure. The book had to be right in front of her. There were lots of news clips from around the globe, an update on a woman in jail for killing her batterer, and a short story about a fat dyke who has to be a bridesmaid in her skinny sister's wedding. What a nightmare. The details were too painful not to be true. All in all, it was shaping up to be a good issue, and from my end it looked pretty mechanical, busy work I could crank out on automatic pilot, giving me plenty of time to think about Chloe, the doctor, and the phone number.

Famous last words.

I was just starting to type in the lead article when I saw the manila envelope. It was right beside the computer, in the no-woman's land between my set-up and the stacking metal bins of the advertising committee. Those women do a hard job well, I'm not complaining, but they tend to spill over into any available space. I'd snagged some yellow plastic tape emblazoned CAUTION! every six inches from a construction site, and glued it to the table where their space ended and mine began. They thought it was cute, but I noticed it was effective. "Don't cross that yellow line," had become a saying amongst us. Probably three years from now, when we were all in law school, married with children or dead, some rendition of *The Women's Page* collective would still be saying it and no one would know why.

Anyway, the manila envelope had a stick-um with my name on it.

Skyler,
How about a "centerfold" of these photos? From the Lesbian/Power Conference.
—Annelise

The quotes around centerfold gave me a bad feeling, but there was no point in putting off the inevitable. I stuck my hand in and pulled out the contents.

Ick, was my first thought. Followed closely by, why me? The third runner-up wasn't a thought really, just a reaction as I spread out the photographs. Terror, grabbing my insides like an orphan, or hunger, or a bird of prey. They'd tied my hands with a belt, just like that. Just like that. And they'd laughed and I think I screamed but I'm not sure. I was fifteen and on my way home from work and there were three of them and the asphalt was so hard, I'd never felt anything so hard as what they did, Beg for it, bitch, the one guy kept saying and nothing's ever been the same since, not really. It was dark, they'd dragged me past the dim circle of light, and there were smashed soda cans and stray tufts of grass breaking through and you don't realize how meaningless clothes are until three boys drag you behind a dumpster and tie your hands with a belt and rip you apart one at a time. If anyone was home across the street, no one cared.

I didn't look at the pictures again. I didn't look at anything for awhile, though I remember putting them back in the envelope and then laying my head on the table. I wanted to scream and I wanted to bleed and I wanted to die and nothing was real. I couldn't feel my hands and feet, I couldn't find the world. My old therapist's voice was suddenly speaking. It's called dissociation, Skyler. Oh, yeah.

Eventually rage kicked in, sealing me off from the gray world. The Land of Lost Meaning, I wanted to joke, except it wasn't funny. And I still had the meeting to get through.

Annelise didn't waste any time. She'd probably been fantasizing about it all day. The thought made me feel even sicker. It was gonna be one great big scene, and just for the record, I wasn't consenting.

"Where's the centerfold? Didn't you get the pictures?" she asked. And then sat back and waited.

We're about the same age and both white but that's where the similarities end. She's way middle-class with a brand new degree from someplace ritzy. It might have been Smith, but I make a point of forgetting information like that. Call it class warfare. Anyway, she's average height and very thin and thinks she's tough and rad because she wears big black boots. Ooh, I'm impressed. It was hate at first sight. She's queer where I'm lesbian, which is to say, through and through. This wasn't our first scuffle but it looked like it was going to be our biggest. I hated the look in her eye, her satiation beginning already.

"I didn't make a 'centerfold.' I don't want to put those pictures in," I said as emotionlessly as possible. I up-ended the envelope and let the pictures tumble down, burnt leaves, acid rain, the nuclear fall-out of woman-hatred.

One by one, the other five women picked them up. I heard Sherry make an angry noise. Sherry's African-American. Her mother mopped white people's floors to put her through school. Put it this way: she doesn't particularly care for Annelise. I'd been praying she'd be on my side.

The four white women didn't say a word. I wasn't sure who I could count on. Georgia was a lesbian in her forties. She was a nurse and a mother and had lots of gray hair to show for it. I didn't know where she stood.

Sarah was our token straight girl, a red diaper baby born into a long and venerable line of Jewish activists. She could name them all, too, who had fought, who had escaped, who had died for what cause. "Did I ever tell you how my Great-Aunt Sophie smuggled guns for the Bolsheviks?" she'd start, and it would be a true story, too, full of history and characters and irony. Her stories always left you wondering if maybe there wasn't some guiding hand of God behind the scenes somewhere. "So," she always ended with a little shrug. I loved her accent, Brooklyn through and through, and she thought mine was kinda cute.

"Skyler, if only you were just a little older," she'd flirt, waiting for my response.

"And you were a lesbian," I'd finish and we'd grin.

Anna was bisexual and liberal and I liked her but I was afraid. She was groovy and anti-militarist and rabidly vegetarian. She had long brown hair and blue eyes and she was proud to say that she'd never once shaved her legs. So what would she think about women taking razors to each others skin and calling it sex? I didn't know which would win out, her liberal tendencies or her radical peacefulness.

And then there was Sally, who was academic in a lesbian Ph.D. kind of way. She was fat and very political about it. You couldn't mistake her for anything but a dyke and I like that in a woman. She could be sarcastic when it suited but she usually listened first. She'd called herself a separatist in years gone by, but there were separatists who were into sado-masochism, so I just didn't know.

Sarah's lip curled in distaste and it registered somewhere in my brain. I took a deep breath.

"That's censorship," Annelise said, leaning back and hanging one arm over the back of her chair. She was having the time of her life.

"It's self-defense," I replied. "We're surrounded by women being tortured and brutalized."

"But this is women taking power over their victimization," she said with a pouty smile.

"No, it's women victimizing other women. 'Taking power' would be smashing the systems that create torture, like male supremacy and racism and imperialism," I replied, mimicking her goading tone.

"Skyler, why are you so disturbed by women's sexuality?" This was her foreplay and I didn't want to play but the only way I knew to stop it was with words.

"I'm disturbed, Annelise, by women training themselves to get off on sadism and cruelty and pain. I'm disturbed that women aren't resisting the basic dynamic of oppression or trying to create something different."

"Maybe we don't want to resist. Maybe we're tired of the patriarchy telling us to say no to sex."

"Men aren't telling you to say no. They don't let you say no."

She snorted and shook her head. Then she leaned forward, lips parting.

"Why don't you admit you want it, Skyler? Just a little?"

That was the moment she'd been waiting for, her thrust, right there. Rape, I thought, this is a form of rape, and five women are watching and no one cares.

"When I was a teenager," I heard a voice, small and faraway, it had to be mine, I could feel the air in my throat, "I had a lot of violent sexual fantasies. Rape fantasies. Like a lot of women. And then I was raped. Really raped. Three guys in a parking lot, on my way home from work. And you know what? I haven't had a rape fantasy since. 'Cause it's not a fantasy and it's not a game and neither is this, Annelise, and I'm telling you 'no.' Can you understand, No? No? Can you?" My voice had grown softer and softer in fury and now it was almost a whisper, I was almost a whisper, just a sound that the wind makes, just a small piece of breath that disappears.

Nobody said a word. Annelise's eyes were bored and pitying. I looked away because it made me want to hit her, to shake her, to scream until she heard and the urge was making me sick. I looked down at the photographs spread out across the table. On top was one I hadn't seen. I stared.

"The last time I heard," I said, breaking the silence with slow, steady words, just follow your heartbeat, this can't go on forever, "this," I said, picking up the picture, "this," I repeated, "was called a swastika."

A woman was hurting another woman and I don't want to say how but one of the spectators had an armband and on it was a swastika.

Annelise's eyes glanced over it.

"We don't have to print that one. There's ten others."

You are out of your fucking mind, I wanted to scream, but I didn't have to.

"Are you crazy?" Sarah demanded. "This is disgusting! First you tell Skyler that she wants to be raped and then you want to publish photographs of lesbians pretending to be Nazis? Nazis?"

The outrage was such a relief, I felt tears gathering strength in my eyes. Water me, my grief, I wanted to plead. Get me home alive.

"I don't want anything to do with this," Sherry added, shaking her head. I knew her word would carry the most weight and I didn't want to tokenize but maybe it should. Maybe the descendants of slaves should have the final say. Maybe that was justice somehow or maybe it was just a no-win situation or maybe it was too complicated and I could think about it later. I shut my eyes and waited for it to be over.

"That's censorship," Annelise repeated, dismissive and angry 'cause we'd taken away her fun.

"Well, no," said Sally. "That's a very glib reading of the meaning of political power. Women don't hold positions of structural power or control the mass media."

"Fine," she said, scooping up her pictures and rolling her eyes. "Don't print them. All my friends were right."

Nobody took the bait. Georgia looked unhappy and Anna hadn't looked up yet. I wanted to feel something, the hard chair or the wooden floor or the weight of flesh on my bones but nothing came through. Except a small, hard fist in my chest. Was it called a heart? I wanted a bath, no lights except faded sun, behind a door that locked, and then I wanted sleep, a long stretch of unconsciousness, days of it, years, more, what would I find when I woke? That the earth was covered in vines, in dark forests and deer prints and I was the only human left? No, it would be piles of refuse, steel bridges, rain that burned over deserts of dead mushrooms, the end had come, the boys had had their way, stripping the rest of us raw, the earth, the sky, the waters, the women, while the lesbians had stood back and laughed.

I watched my hands, willing them to move.

"This is probably something the whole collective needs to talk about," said Georgia.

I don't want to go through this again, I wanted to say, and realized that I had.

Georgia blinked.

"You shouldn't have to," Sarah added quickly. I could see her concern but I couldn't feel it.

"So now we're not even allowed to talk about it?" Annelise sneered.

"Oh, we're gonna talk about it," Sarah replied, staring her down. "But there's going to be some serious ground rules. Like some basic feminist principles about respect and boundaries and women's sexual integrity."

I felt myself standing up. Something else had taken over, some animal instinct of self-preservation, coupling emotional shut-down with physical action. Just get the fuck out of here. Knapsack. Keys. Bike. Home. Before the asphalt is all you feel. The noose of leather, a strip of dead flesh choking your hands, and then what they did and the smell of hatred, of male sweat and beer and female blood and the way they laughed. Then the sound of their footsteps as they ran away and I was all alone and I cried because I couldn't get the belt undone. But I used my teeth, the cold metal in my mouth and the stars were cold and the ground was cold and the blue light from the television across the street was so, so cold. I started shaking, remembering that cold as I stood at the table nine years later. Hate. I hated Annelise. Everyone was staring, not knowing what to do.

I slipped my backpack over one shoulder.

"Are you leaving?" Sarah asked ineffectually.

I couldn't answer. I only had one word left, that one human word of reasons and choices and meanings.

"Why?" I asked, looking at Annelise. "Why?"

Her lip curled in distaste, her eyes blank and empty. She looked ugly, ugly and stupid, and if she understood the question, she didn't have an answer.

"She doesn't know why, Skyler," Judith said, her own sadness heavy as a sleeping child. "That doesn't make her less accountable, but she doesn't know. If she did, she wouldn't be able to do it. Unless she was a real libertine. But then I'd call her a sociopath."

"Except it's so normal," I said, my voice a flat sound in a flat world. I held the phone tighter, imagining those long thin wires stretched over miles of hills and into mountains where women lived together. A barn and a house and a little girl. The wild roses and the way the air smelled after the rain. And Judith.

"It's fun being a feminist, isn't it?" she said. Her voice was too sweet for sarcasm and so she just sounded sad instead.

"I can see why everyone gives up. It's like when they do tests on college guys and they all score somewhere on the hate index when it comes to women. Half of them think we want to be raped and the other half think we deserve it. What the fuck is Annelise talking about? Like rape is some kind of new, hip idea?" Tears were burning in my eyes. Why do some tears hurt and other tears release hurt? "Or like that psychologist who did tests on Nazi war criminals and they all came out normal. Perfectly normal."

"In a perfectly sadistic world," Judith added like an echo, softer, fewer edges, would it eventually just be sound, without words or intent, just a human sound like any other? Would it always be like this?

"I wish I was dead," I said, shutting my eyes tight.

"Skyler?" she said, all caution and concern.

"No, I'm not gonna kill myself," I reassured her. "I just wish I wasn't alive. You know the difference?" I tried to imagine her arms around me, tried to imagine that I'd wanted to kiss her or anyone once, that connection had been possible and desire a state of grace.

"I think so. You're having a bad time. You know it won't last, right? Can you tell yourself that it won't go on forever?"

"It won't go on forever," I repeated, making her laugh.

"Why don't you come out for a visit? I'm too busy this weekend, but what are you doing next weekend?"

Nothing, I almost said in a burst of pure longing.

"Not much," I said instead, trying to sound casual and failing. I gave up. "I want to see you so bad. Everything sucks, Judith. Everything."

"Come out next Saturday, then. It'd be good to see you again," she urged.

My heart raised its weary head and thumped its tail at the tone. We finished making plans and I hung up. There was something here, I knew it. I didn't care what she told herself. I was going to get her to fall in love with me if it killed me.

SIXTEEN

It was Thursday morning. I stared at the phone and then at the number and then back at the phone. I'd checked in with my three partners in crime but nobody had had any brilliant ideas about what to actually do with the phone number of the evil doctor. I needed his address and I needed to know if Chloe was there. I also needed to know if he'd killed Diane Frasier, was a conduit for illegal drugs, or knew anything about any of the above. Okay, if I could just get his address that would be something.

I picked up the phone and dialed. It rang once, then twice. Maybe he'd already left for work. Three times. Did his wife work?

"Hello?" said a female voice, as if on cue, brisk and efficient.

"Good morning, Ma'am. My name is Pam West and I'm with the Media Research Center and we're doing a survey this morning about television viewing habits. The survey should take less than five minutes and to thank you for your time we'll send you coupons worth $500 for some nationally known products that every household can use. So if I may, Ma'am, I'd like to ask, how many adults live at your residence?"

"Well, I'd like to help. My daughter did phone surveys one summer, but this isn't my residence. I work here. I'm the housekeeper."

"That's perfectly fine, Ma'am," I reassured her, trying to keep my voice smooth and neutral when I felt like singing. Piece of cake. This was going to be a piece of cake. The Unsuspecting Housekeeper instead of the Doctor of Evil Deeds. Oh, yes. "If you could just answer as many of the questions as you can, that will be very helpful. How many adults live at the residence where you are employed?"

"Two," she answered. God, people are so gullible it's sad.

"And how many of them are employed outside the home?"

"Both of them."

"And are those two male or female?"

"One of each," she laughed. "It's the doctor and his wife."

"And how many newspapers does the household subscribe to?"

"They get the Boston paper every day and *The New York Times* on Sundays."

"And how many magazines would you estimate they subscribe to?"

"Oh," she said, considering, "hmm . . ."

I let her take as much time as she wanted. I didn't want to get to the punchline too quick. I tried to conjure up a picture of her. Did she wear a uniform? She was white and she had gray hair that she was tired of dyeing and glasses for reading. Her voice sounded solid and in my mind her body matched, a soon-to-be grandmother with a safe, soft lap. But who knew.

"I'd say five. But that doesn't count the medical journals that the Doctor gets. I don't know about those, only the ones I see around the house. *Time* and *House and Garden,* like that."

"That's fine, Ma'am. We don't need to know about professional journals. And how many children are in the household?'

"Well," and here she hesitated and I held my breath, "there's a little girl staying here. Both her parents died and Dr. Gunther's her guardian. It's sad, that's hard on a child."

Her guardian? Fucking shit. How'd that happened? And how could I fit the orphan's legal status into my television survey? I couldn't think fast enough and it was getting me confused. Could I ask? No, better to go for broke on the address. Luckily I'd made notes.

"How many hours of unsupervised television would you estimate the child watches?"

"That I don't. I haven't had that much to do with her. She's in daycare, so my guess is not a lot."

"You've been very helpful, Ma'am. That's all the questions we have today. We'd like to send you our coupon packet as a way of saying thank you. If I could have the address there . . ." My heart began to gear up as I said the last sentence.

"So the Gunthers get them and not me?" she demanded in a friendly way.

"I see your point, Ma'am," I replied, thinking on my feet. "Tell you what. Give me your address as well and I'll make sure you get a packet, too."

Come on, come on. Just give me the fucking address.

"All right. The Gunther's address is 131—"

And here her voice suddenly ended. I heard her make a startled noise and then the phone sounded like it was being manhandled and then another voice was in my ear. Not a nice voice. Not one bit nice. Doctor Gunther's.

"Who is this?" he demanded quietly, more a threat than a question.

"Hello, Sir," I said, adopting my pleasant, neutral phone survey voice. "My name is Pam West and I'm with the Media Research Center in Baltimore, Maryland—" Baltimore? Maryland? "—and your housekeeper has been very helpful answering questions for our research on television viewing habits. As our way of saying thank you we have a coupon packet worth $500 for nationally-known products that any household could use—"

"We're not interested," he said coldly.

The phone went dead.

God fucking damn it.

I brooded for the rest of the morning, played my bass, ate a piece of toast, and stared at the ceiling. There had to be another point of access to Dr. Gunther. I kept replaying each scene in my mind: the bank machine, the newspaper articles, Diane's purse, the Strausses, Nat's office, the funeral. And now the phone call to his house.

What did I know? Chloe was in his clutches. Okay, but wait. I sat up slowly, staring at the wall now. Why? I'd been going on the theory that he'd made threatening noises about Chloe to get Diane to comply with whatever-was-going-on, and where she was vulnerable was her little girl. But now Diane was dead—murdered—and Gunther had taken possession of the kid. Why? I mean, they bump Diane off because she didn't want to play anymore or she knew too much or something. But why take the kid after Diane's already dead, when Chloe's use as a leverage point was obviously moot?

I felt very sick all of a sudden. What use could they have for a four-year-old child? Why fake someone's suicide? Did Chloe "know too much?" How much could a four-year-old know? And why not just kill her too?

I made a loud moan and held my head in my hands. It felt like it was going to explode. All right, I didn't need to figure it all out. I needed to get a lead on the doctor.

I decided to check the mail. And was not unrewarded. Food stamps had finally arrived. Maybe my luck was starting to break.

Steed and I rode down to the co-op, where I left her leaning lazily against a No Parking sign. I like that in a bike, how she could break rules that a car could ignore only at its peril. The thing about a bike is, you can have it both ways: the perks of being a pedestrian (sidewalks, walk signals at traffic lights, going the wrong way down one-way streets) with the ease of being a car (speed, asphalt, membership in a line of forty mph lumps of steel—a hegemony no one was going to fuck with). Things are more complicated than just sidewalk or street, and I like being able to pick and choose as it suited. A metaphor for my life, I suppose.

My luck continued to hold. Billy was nowhere in sight, the organic broccoli was half price, and the radio was playing an Indigo Girls' song I'd never heard, which could only mean one thing: a new album. Forty-seven government dollars later I had food. Real food. Yummy, filling stuff like pasta and red onions and tofu sausage and peppers and fresh strawberries and garlic cheddar. God, I was hungry. Really, really hungry.

I rode home with my mouth watering, and Chloe,

Annelise, Judith and my mother all on hold. The sky was gray and I could smell the ocean and I wanted to just keep going, to the place where the land ended and the sea began. I wanted to stand there and listen to those lonely birds and then walk for miles, past the last house and the last footprint and the last stupid tin can and find a shell to put to my ear. And there'd be no one there. Eventually I'd leave my shoes, shed my shirt, I'd keep walking and maybe I could cry. The sand would be white and soft and it wouldn't ever end. Then the sun would lower her head and the sky would go pink and orange where she drifted into sleep. Does the sun dream? Then the stars would come, one by one in the purple sky, one by one they'd be fierce and brave until the sky was black and covered with stars and maybe then I could cry. Finally I'd swim. Would the water drown me or hold me and which did I want? Maybe all I knew was that I wanted: water and stars and dark black night and endless sand and lonely, soaring gulls. I wanted and it was enough.

SEVENTEEN

I settled down at my desk, a plate of tofu sausage in hand. I needed a job, which meant I had to write resumes. Just send them out like hopeful homing pigeons to every publication I could think of, maybe they'd roost on someone's desk long enough to be noticed.

I'd brought a fork in with me but it was just for appearances. Eating with my fingers adds something to the experience, touching something warm and fragrant and then you get to put your fingers in your mouth and lick them off. Hey, a little auto-eroticism never hurt anyone.

This time I actually had my newspaper opened to the Help Wanteds when I saw it. A book. Laying on my desk. Innocent enough. Sarah from *The Women's Page* lent it to me. John Stoltenberg, hardback. I hadn't gotten around to it yet. ·All of a sudden it popped into my brain, like a bubble of air rising through water and bursting on the surface.

. . . I've got Rosenberg at 8 AM, fucking faggot Jew, makes me sick . . . My little Fuzzy Friend from Diane's. Rosenberg. I'd bet anything he was a professor and the boy was a student. And I'd bet even more that I could find out where he taught and where the class was. And Fuzz Boy would be there, too. If I went, maybe I could follow him and maybe he would lead me to the Doctor. Maybe that was too many maybes, but maybe I didn't have a choice.

I finished my little morsels lickety-split, and abandoned the paper, a big white mess I'd have to deal with later. I'd have to get a job later, too, I told myself as I hoisted Steed over my shoulder and headed for the street.

Did I already tell you that the BPL will never let you down? My afternoon was no exception. I methodically worked my way through all the Boston area college catalogs, flipping directly to the faculty rosters in the back, which luckily were alphabetical. I tried Northeastern first. Diane had worked there and who knows, maybe there was a connection.

One Eric Rothberg taught in the History Department. I took down the information even though I was 99.9 percent positive that the boy had said Rosenberg. There was nothing even close at B.U., Harvard, or Boston College. But I found him eventually. At M.I.T. He taught math. Daryl Rosenberg, with a Ph.D. in math and another one in logic. Go for it, Daryl.

I took the stairs down to the basement two at a time, thinking almost as fast. If on Sunday, Fuzz Brain had class tomorrow, that meant Monday. So it was probably a MWF deal. Now I just had to get the secretary at the Math Department to tell me where.

I even had a quarter in my pocket. I dropped it in the slot and listened while it ran a quick maze through the machine. Then the dial tone. I was ready. I punched in the number I'd gotten from the catalog and tried to set my mind on students. Overwrought, over-worked, and over-convinced of their own importance.

"Math Department," said a female voice, like it was one word.

"Hi, um, I, like, need to find out where Professor Rosenberg's 8 o'clock class meets on Fridays?" I fished hopefully.

"Go to the registrar's office and look in the class schedule," came the reply.

"Look, I don't live on campus and I owe him an assignment. He said if I dropped it off tomorrow he wouldn't penalize me for lateness, but I don't remember where. I've got a sick two-year-old and I don't have a sitter and I'd have to drag her along on the "T" with me—" I was laying it on thick but it paid off. Maybe sick children trigger some kind of species survival instinct, who knows?

"All right, all right," she said with a sigh. "Can you hold?" she asked and didn't wait for a reply.

I uncapped my pen and held it in a ready position. A bag lady came out of the bathroom and leaned against the wall beneath the "No Loitering" sign. Everything about her was thin, her dirty hair across her vulnerable scalp, the tight skin on her face, the watery cover on her far-away eyes, the stretched handles of her plastic shopping bag. "Palazzi Shoes" it read, gold on white like a wedding invitation. The thinness ended at her feet. Her calves and ankles were huge, rounder almost than her thighs. There were red and purple places where the skin seemed to have worn through. I looked away. A life on the street was a life utterly without privacy. Public bathrooms, public libraries, public streets, and the public gaze of strangers who saw enough to look away.

"All right," a voice said in my ear, "here it is."

"Thank you so much," I answered on automatic, writing down what she told me. All I could see where those terrible legs.

She hung up without replying.

I stuck the scrap of paper in my back pocket and thought about my wallet. I had nothing but food stamps. No. I had three years of college and a roof. A nice roof. It didn't leak and it held in the heat and the floor kept my bed up, which was soft and safe. The bag lady hadn't moved. I took out $10 in food stamps and went over to her.

"Hi," I said.

She looked me in the eye but I don't know what she saw.

"For you," I said, holding out my hand.

She didn't respond. I bent down and laid them at her feet. Then I walked away.

EIGHTEEN

"Maybe he's the kids real father or something," Amy said, lounging full-length on the couch while I brought out dinner. "You need some help?"

"Nah. You do this all day. Don't worry about it," I replied, setting down a pot of herbed rice. The smell of basil hit my nose on its way up to heaven. Mmm. Next came a plate of tofu balls, a green salad, and a small pot of vegetarian gravy. Even Amy looked impressed.

"Skyler, I'm touched," she said, taking a seat at the table.

"Yo, Jaye!" I hollered down the hall. "Dinner's ready."

I like our living room/dining room set up. We have four wooden chairs that match and a wooden table that doesn't, but that's okay. There's an old couch with medieval looking upholstery, dark green with white and purple flowers, and deer—I like the deer—but it's fading fast. On the wall above is a poster that was actually wrapping paper. The World Tree, surrounded by a circle of animals and a moon and sun with faces, all painted in bright and shiny primaries. There's a little fox that's particularly endearing. This room also has the most windows and the days were getting longer all the time.

"Listen, I notice how you guys feed me when the money runs out. Anyway, my brain was all over the place with this Chloe stuff—"

"Skyler and the Missing Child," Jaye put in as she took her seat. "God, this looks great."

"So, Amy, what's your theory?" I asked, carrying a trembling spoonful of gravy to my plate.

"What if this Dr. Gunther is really Chloe's father? Maybe Diane had an affair with him. Or maybe they were married and Jonathan was husband number two. It could all be about a custody battle."

"So, he's into control and ownership," Jaye said thoughtfully, while she methodically speared a tofu ball. I watched her raise it to her mouth. It's that gray area between friends and sex, that huge, wild land that lesbians lay claim to. Putting her shoes on, her black canvas sneakers; folding her laundry; making coffee in the morning with sleep still bending her hair sideways and the smell of the fresh coffee beans, vanilla, mocha, almond. It was the way she inhabited her life that I wanted to bear witness to, a hunger for her presence that was almost sex, except we didn't touch. Through the eyes of the world, she was not beautiful, her face too flat and boyish, clipped hair a screaming assault on femininity, but I looked and saw something else entirely. A woman in possession of her soul, who would smile only when she meant it and was not afraid.

"So maybe he's been stalking her," Amy added, spooning more rice onto her plate.

"Okay, it might fit. She was definitely scared the moment he walked into the bank kiosk. Then the first drug set-up would have been to try to prove her an unfit mother. Okay, and maybe," I was getting excited, "maybe he found out she was about to skip town, so he killed her."

"And took the kid," Jaye finished.

"So what about the will? And what about the Strausses?"

"Maybe it's really Nathan's kid," Amy said. We ignored her.

"All right, try this," Jaye continued. "What if Chloe was an heir to something he wanted? That would bring in the will. Nat could have been Diane's lawyer. I mean, if the kid's an heir to something big, you'd need a lawyer. And an accountant."

"I still think Nathan's the father," Amy said, chewing her rice with an innocent expression. We both looked at her.

"Well, why not? Then it would be just like one of those nighttime soaps. Remember Dallas?"

Sometimes I think Amy's from another solar system.

The phone rang and Jaye got up to get it.

"Actually," I said, "Nathan did have a box of condoms in his desk at the office. He's obviously up to something."

"But who believes me?" Amy sighed, taking another bite of rice.

"What if Diane and Nathan were having an affair?" I asked. Amy stared back at me, eyes narrowing in thought.

"You said he had a file with the news clippings about her death," she pointed out. She sat up straight. "God, maybe he killed her."

"Skyler," Jaye said in a low voice, suddenly beside me. "It's your mother. Are you home?"

Great. I put my hand on my forehead and pulled down the length of my face. Why does that feel so good when you're totally frustrated?

"Yeah, I'll take it," and even I heard the dread under my monotone. What was it, 6:30 PM? Would she be drunk yet?

I walked down the hall, leaving behind food and friends. It was dark in the hall and I wanted to turn the light on but somehow the impulse got backed up in my brain, a grid lock of conflict: love, fear, anger, at her, at me, at the cowardice that I knew would win, and an overwhelming surge of thick sleepiness, a self-protective gesture, like covering your head under a blow.

I picked up the phone and wondered what my mouth would say and if the rest of me would agree.

"Hi, Ma," I heard myself start, tone dead neutral.

"Skyler, you haven't called all week. I was starting to worry about you," she said, but what she meant was, why wasn't I worried about her.

"I've been worried about you too," I said in that same slow tone, plenty of space between the words but she wasn't about to fill it in.

"Well, I'm glad to hear that my only daughter cares enough to worry. Maybe she could care enough to call."

It would be easy to coast into mother-daughter talk, all I had to do was hold still and she'd do the rest, the conversation would follow its usual path, like an instinctive migration to the Arctic and back: her asshole boss, stories from her friends, news about family. I could hold still and just listen, laugh occasionally when a pause came up like a cue card, pack my heart on ice and send it off to cold storage. Or maybe I could just bury it as deep as I could dig. Could I leave it behind or would it lie in wait, or would it burrow back up toward the light? Would it track me down by my scent or would my fame precede me: The Woman Without a Heart? Would I come home late one night and find it, beating placidly on my bed, I'm here! thump, thump, I found you! Was there any way out?

"I went to work this week, thanks for asking," she started. I heard her take a drag on her cigarette. Now, I thought. Say it. But my mouth didn't move.

"While I was gone they went no-smoking, right? They wait until I'm in the hospital—practically on my death bed—to pull this one. You know who did it. It's that bitch Sharon. She's a vegetarian. Like you," she added this last as if she was conceding a point.

There was another second of silence while she sucked air through her cigarette. Her reference to me meant I could respond here if I wanted. Defend my pacifism or my honor or refute her correlation between vegetarians and no-smoking policies. Engage, that's what she wanted. Argue. Show her that she'd found an in and wounded enough to make you block and parry. Still, I said nothing, buried alive by silence.

"So when I need to smoke, I have to go downstairs and outside. Outside. Just to smoke a goddamn cigarette. So I asked Mr. Callachi, 'What am I supposed to do when it rains? What about when it's snowing, which it will be doing again before you know it?' And he says he'll get back to me. And somebody even put this big sign up in the ladies room. Please do not smoke thank you. Thank you for nothing."

"Maybe you should stop," I was saying without thinking. Maybe, Ma, maybe?

"Oh, Skyler, please. Don't start."

But once I'd started, I couldn't stop. I opened my mouth and there it was, like something being born and it was way too late to stop it, all I could do was bear down and feel my insides coming out with a life all their own and hope it would be okay. Hope like women have always hoped, for some blessed mercy in our travail, borne all in the name of love.

"Have you stopped drinking yet? Ma?"

"Don't start with me, Skyler. Don't start," she said, a double-bladed knife, and I didn't care except my heart wanted out, it was pounding so hard, do hearts bruise, just another muscle? Would it be black and blue and sullen inside my ribs tomorrow? I can't let you go yet, I wanted to whisper to it, please stay. Meanwhile my mouth kept moving.

"You're an alcoholic, Ma. And if you don't face it, you're going to kill yourself." The words were slow, like the end of a story, the last line where it all suddenly matters, or the end of the day and the lullaby that lets you let it go, slipping into sleep. I meant her no harm.

She slammed the phone down and I was left holding the receiver, an umbilical cord to nowhere. I put it back in its cradle and felt myself rising. I was glad I hadn't turned the lights on. Down the hall was silence.

"She hung up on me," I called to Amy and Jaye.

I saw their little faces poke around the corner, all sympathy. It made me laugh.

"It's okay, you guys," I said, closing the distance, coming back into the gold light of evening. "She can drink herself to death for all I care."

I didn't want to talk about it anymore. I wanted everything to be normal, just a regular dinner between friends, just a bunch of average lesbians having a chat and I wanted them to stop looking at me like somebody had died or something. I sat back in my chair and shrugged at them. If they didn't start acting normal, I was going to start screaming.

"Did you figure it out yet?" I asked conversationally. I would feel better after I ate. I dumped another blob of rice in my plate.

"No," said Amy, following my lead onto safer ground. "But I've been thinking. We did so well at Nathan's office, why not have a go at the good doctor's old workplace? The Fertility Palace, or whatever it's called?"

"You're a few millennia off," Jaye smirked. "What is

it called?"

"The Reproductive Health Center at Boston General," I supplied. Something was bothering me as I said it, like an itch in my brain that I couldn't get in to scratch. "You want to stage another break in?"

"The first one went so well," Amy said apologetically.

"Hospitals are open twenty-four hours a day. It might not be that hard," Jaye said slowly, while I swallowed some water. And again, and again. As long as no one noticed I'd be fine. I put the glass down and made myself scoop up some rice.

"The doctor I talked to had Gunther's phone number somewhere at hand. The address is probably right there with it," I said. I stuck the rice in my mouth and started to chew. I was afraid the smell would be too strong, afraid of the revolt spreading from mouth on down, working its way through the ranks, a domino theory of digestion. But it was actually okay. Hunger had defeated the emotional uprising, isn't that the way of it. I took another bite.

"So let's say we get his address. Then what?" asked Jaye as I watched her, her white button-down shirt as neat as when she left this morning. I'd take off clothes like that before I ate, but not Jaye. There wasn't a grain out of place. I wanted that clean, clear clarity, the sparseness of white without wrinkles or the lingering imprint of food long eaten; the same kind of shoes, year in, year out, like she always knew where she was headed. I wanted to be Jaye, not me, not today anyway. It was stupid but there it was.

"Yeah, then what?" Amy repeated. They were both looking at me.

"I don't know. Kidnap her? Yeah, right. I guess we're going to have to get evidence of something, enough evidence to make sure he gets busted. For whatever."

"If we just knew what whatever was," Amy added, contemplating her last spoonful of rice.

"There's always murder," I replied. The food was helping, but only marginally. I could still feel that watery sense of unreality taking over, which made anything possible. Plates could go flying, people could start crying, doors could slam and slam and slam, and the only safe place was somewhere small. Under the table, at the back of the closet, curled up beneath the covers in the dark.

"You guys up for a break-in at the hospital?" I asked point blank.

"Sure," said Jaye with a shrug.

"Absolutely," Amy added.

"How about Saturday?" I suggested.

"Katie'll be out of town," Amy said.

We all considered for a minute.

"Why is she the only one of us with a girlfriend?" Jaye grumbled good-naturedly.

"Gotta be the accent," Amy insisted.

"That and those baby-blue eyes," I added. "I don't think there'll be much to scale, I mean it's basically a big block of cement. Wanna try without her?"

They both nodded.

"Okay, it's a date," I said. I swallowed a bite of salad and the vinegar burned like tears. I wanted the sensation to last, the pain almost a relief, and I remembered Morgan, a lover I'd had in college. Who cut herself. Every time we got in bed all she could think about were the hands that had been there before mine. Her father, her uncle, her uncle's business partner. They'd passed her around like beer or cigarettes, something consumable and cheap and inanimate. She had straight dark hair and huge gray eyes and there are some things I will never understand. How anyone could do that to a child? Why? What's the reason? Where's the pleasure in the hatred? I don't know when I realized she was cutting, but I remember finding her in the bathroom, blood as dark as her hair in the dim light, spilling over the soft skin of her arms, her eyes all sleepy and dull, the pain was her drug and she'd had her fix. I bandaged her arms and she let me and I prayed. Catholic girl to the end, I called up every female saint I knew and I prayed for Morgan, and then I went for Mary and prayed for those men to die.

I took a swallow of water and pushed my plate

away, salad unfinished. Jaye was watching me and pretending not to. I stood up.

"Give me your plates," I said, trying for a reasonable tone. They did as told and I left for the kitchen. In a moment I heard them talking but I couldn't catch the words under the sound of running water. Warm water, clean and clear, to take away all remnants of the past, and I wanted to cry and I didn't.

NINETEEN

I'd never strolled the grounds at M.I.T. but it was about what I'd expected. The buildings were clean and shiny and the students looked like they'd stepped out of a J. Crew catalog. There's something enlightening about seeing hordes of middle class plus people, the smoothness of unworried skin, the teeth they take for granted, the ease with which everything comes. I didn't look out of place particularly, I just knew I didn't belong.

I'd photocopied the map from the catalog at the BPL and I'd circled my destination in red the night before. Sometimes it helps feeling competent and organized. The building wasn't hard to find. I hitched up my knapsack and entered therein.

Room 110 was where it belonged, right after 109. I peeked in through the window and what I saw made me want to high-five the door frame: a large room with a slightly sloping floor and rows and rows of chairs. Oh, sweet anonymity. No one would notice and no one would care. I slipped inside and took an aisle seat in the back.

It was a quarter of and there were only three students, heads bent to notebooks as if in prayer. I could hear the soft scratching of a pencil from the nearest one, a short, skinny white guy with black, black hair, so intent on his calculations he didn't notice my scrutiny. Was there a passion for math like music or art or love? Was he up at night making beauty in a universe of pure numbers? He still hadn't noticed me.

I took a notebook out of my knapsack and scrounged around in the depths for a pen. Shit. Should I have brought a pencil instead? A faux pas among the math nerds. God, would anyone notice? A few more students trickled in, some of them looking decidedly slept on. I opened my notebook and started writing random phrases for camouflage.

7:50 AM. Suddenly there were students in droves. I didn't want to keep looking behind me, but looking forward all I could see were the backs of heads. I figured I could still spot him. So far there hadn't been any crew cuts.

At 7:55 AM I was starting to get antsy. Maybe I'd had too many "maybe's" on this trajectory, I mean, Rosenberg was a common enough name, plus who knew if I'd even heard the little schmuck right.

But then I saw his head, bobbing down the aisle as fuzzy as you please. He picked a row in the middle of the room and got himself settled. About then the professor came in, too, and probably a hundred more students and everybody had about sixty seconds to find their friends, fill them in on whatever important events had happened since they'd last talked, and grab a seat. It was loud and crowded but not threatening. Just overwhelming. I remembered one of the reasons I'd hated school. It was always like this in a crowd of people, this dissipation of myself, like my mouth was sealing over and retreating behind my teeth from the sheer pressure of the noise. Everyone was laughing and chatting and basically being friends and I was on the outside, way outside, looking in. I scribbled more nonsense in my notebook and tried to pretend my face wasn't hot. Why does everything humiliate me?

"Okay," called the professor, Dr. Rosenberg I presumed. "Settle down. This is our last class before exams, so we need to get started."

So they settled down, and surprisingly quickly. People are so malleable. Always willing to do as told if spoken to with authority. I mean this wasn't like an airplane crash, "Please fasten your seat belts and extinguish all smoking materials, we're expecting some turbulent calculations ahead." But in ten seconds they were all seated and silent.

Whatever it was he was talking about was way over my head. I'd gotten up to trigonometry in high school, and I'd really done okay in it, but it just wasn't my thing. I tried to pay attention to Dr. Daryl. There were lots of x's and y's, surprise surprise, and his inflection changed about as much as the laws of the universe. My attention stuck for about sixty seconds, before cutting its moorings and heading for uncharted waters.

The room was warm from lots of human bodies

and institutional habit, and the professor's voice went on and on. My eyelids started to be an effort, huge, heavy things I had to put down. When my head started following I gave up. I curled my arms up on the fold-down desk and tucked my weary head safely inside.

It wasn't a deep sleep, but I started dreaming almost instantly. Diane Frasier's dead body was on the floor in my mother's living room. Around her, eight babies were crawling, her babies, they were hungry and didn't understand. I was in the kitchen. On the table was a roasted turkey, its skin all brown and shiny. Arranged around it were cutting and cooking implements. There was something so repulsive about the whole scene. Soon the babies would find the turkey and eat it. They were making little mewing and cooing noises, like small animals. Working on instinct, they'd find the food. The smell of it was making me sick. I could hear them coming toward the kitchen on soft baby knees and feet. I felt so, so sick.

I woke with a jerk, and hoped I hadn't made any noise. No one was looking at me so I figured I hadn't. I was sweaty and hot and I really really wanted a drink of water but I didn't want to be conspicuous, so I stayed put. I also didn't want to fall asleep again. I picked up my pen and starting writing, hoping the activity would clear up my grogged-out brain.

What sucks, I titled a column, underlining the words with three crooked lines. My mother, I wrote beneath it. Diane's murder. Chloe's in danger. Annelise and her icky friends. No job. Judith's not in love.

Judith. Next weekend I'd see her. The thought was all longing with no substance, like a heavy load with nowhere to set it. I could feel my heart opening like a rocky gorge and I was starting to fall. I changed the subject.

Minnesota. There was a cheery thought. I hadn't ever been, but Jaye and Katie both had. Not as performers, though. They were expecting 8,000 women—wimmin—this year. It was gonna be huge. I glanced at my watch. 8:45 AM. God, wasn't this ever going to be over? Did anybody really care what this guy was saying? In front of me, a line of young, jersied arms busily took notes. I guess so.

Okay, another list. Things to take to Minnesota. I underlined this one four times and added an exclamation point. Toothbrush was my number one item. Face it, Gabriel, deep down, you're boring.

At 8:50 AM exactly, as if moved by some invisible biological clue—amount of sun, change in temperature, the swelling of a faraway tide—everyone closed their books and opened their mouths. There was a small rush on the professor. I kept a casual eye on the progress of my nasty, brutish, and short friend. He was making his way quickly up the aisle. I pretended to be engrossed in Mr. Double Doctorate's final calculations, until Fuzz Boy was almost beside me. Then I shut my notebook, stood up, and slid into the swell of students. I was two bodies behind him. Not bad.

He hung a left in the hall and I followed, keeping a buffer zone of two or three future nuclear scientists between us. What else do people learn at places like this, bridge building? My heart was going quick from all the excitement. I was 100 percent certain he wasn't onto me.

At the end of the hall, he stopped before a well-used bulletin board. I slowed my pace and hung back against the wall behind him. It was all right, there were hordes of people by then, rushing madly to their B.S.'s. Fuzz Boy tacked a flyer up. I saw it white against layers of colored paper, but I didn't have a chance to read it. He was off and I was in pursuit. He turned the corner into the lobby and I tried to follow, but a huge crowd of students came pouring out of the auditorium and, I'm ashamed to say it, I lost him. He could have gone out the doors, around the next corner, up the stairs, into the elevator, or to the men's room. I stood immobilized, counting off the seconds, while I looked the lobby over and over. People pushed by me like salmon desperate to spawn. The noise of feet and chatter was overwhelming, but I couldn't see him anywhere. God damn it. I circled around to the doors and stepped out into the cool air, scanning the human horizon. Still nothing. I ducked back in and went around to the stairwell. If he'd gone in there he was long gone. The pace was definitely fast. I watched for a second as a series of jock boys took the stairs two at a time. Maybe that was how they got their aerobic exercise. I ducked back out into the lobby. The crowd was starting to thin, but it was too late. I'd lost my man. And that was the last class of the semester. Shit.

My only hope was the flyer he'd posted. I found it easily on the bulletin board, but I immediately wished I hadn't. It was for a meeting of the Christian Fellowship of M.I.T. New members were always welcome and it was tonight.

There was no way out of it. Just what I wanted to do with my Friday evening. I headed outside. I could feel a decidedly foul mood coming on, and even the spring air didn't help. I thought about what to wear the whole way home.

TWENTY

I was going to have to go in drag and, considering the length of my hair, it was going to have to be male. God, I hate gender. Don't get me wrong, I'm female through and through and I'll cast my lot with women each and every time. But that means facing who's doing what to whom, i.e., men, hurting, and women, respectively.

Like when I use a public bathroom and all the women look at me in horror and inform me that this is the ladies' room. No really? I want to respond, extra-heavy on the sarcasm. And then, What's it to you?

But I know what it is to them. If I was a man, it'd be a violation, a physical threat, and potential violence. I know better than they know and isn't that the irony. Usually I just say, "Don't worry, I'm a woman," as matter-of-factly as I can. I try not to fade into one of those publicly humiliated smiles and I try not to stutter. Meantime, they just keep staring.

"What do Christians wear?" Jaye had pondered with me. That's after she finished laughing. All I could picture were those Mormon types, always in dark suits with white shirts and skinny ties. Neither of us owned anything like that, but that was just as well since it probably wouldn't have been appropriate.

"Casual, but neat," Jaye had advised. "And here," she said, tossing me an ace bandage from her top drawer. "You might want that."

So there I was in front of another M.I.T. building, this one modern gray and ugly. I was wearing, starting from the top, my denim jacket, a white button-down shirt, a blue t-shirt, and the ace bandage. My breasts aren't that big to start with, so under all that they were invisible. I'd worn my baggiest jeans and my sneakers, wish they were newer but oh well.

"You look great," Jaye had encouraged with a smirk. "Don't do anything I wouldn't do."

"Like pray?"

"Like pick up any Christian girls."

It was seven on the dot as I walked toward the

room. Rhymes with doom, I thought glumly. My footsteps echoed a tiny bit, the sound lingering in the hall. There were empty rooms with open doors on either side of me, all dark, except for the last bit of sun. I could hear voices down the hall and I couldn't believe I was going to go through with this. What's the worst thing that could happen? I revved myself up. Someone could say, Excuse me, I think you're a woman dressed like a man? So what? So then I leave. It's not like they're gonna kill me or even arrest me, I repeated severely while I made the final turn into the room. I could feel the sweat backing up under my ace bandage. I had arrived.

Six expectant faces turned to look at me. There were four women and two guys and one of them was mine.

"Hello, welcome," said the other boy. His smile was the kind that the words "in perpetuity" apply to. It wasn't vapid, but it wasn't real either. Just always there, an outward and visible sign of an inward and spiritual broken record. Jesus saves. Smile, God loves you.

"My name's Matthew," he continued, holding out his hand.

Of course it is and if it wasn't you'd probably have changed it so it was.

"Hi," I replied, matching him smile for smile, our arms pumping in unison. "My name's Jonah."

Once it was out of my mouth I couldn't believe I'd said it. Where do you dream these things up, Gabriel? Jonah? Could you get anymore Old Testament? Why not Ezekiel while you're at it? Maybe I felt like I was about to be swallowed by something huge, and I only had one quick question: Did Jonah live through the experience?

"Welcome," he said again, then turned to the rest. "It's about seven. Should we get started?"

The chairs were in a circle, the women were all in skirts and everyone was white.

"Let's bow our heads in prayer," said Matthew. Everyone took a seat and one more Christian arrived. My fuzzy friend seemed happy to see him.

"Hey, John," he said, even though everyone had bowed their heads already. John raised a finger in greeting and slipped into an empty chair.

"If we could bow our heads," Matthew repeated. I got the feeling there were chronic male turf battles here. Testosterone for Jesus.

I bowed my head, shut my eyes, and tried to look pious. There was a minute of silence. I could feel how my posture had changed, being male. I didn't exactly sit up straighter, it was more like sitting up bigger. There was more room, more latitude, more air filling out my ribs when I breathed, and my feet felt firmer on the ground. I wondered if I was cute, as a boy.

"Oh, Lord," Matthew began, "we humbly pray for your forgiveness."

I turned off faster than you can say "recovering Catholic." My mom wasn't that big on religion—I think getting pregnant and thrown out of the house at seventeen probably had something to do with it—but it was enough. Church was a sporadic activity when I was a kid. First communion but never confirmed about sums it up. I hated it. The nuns were nasty, the priests were domineering, the torture scenes done in stained glass were icky, and God was everywhere and wanted me to feel guilty. Plus the kids who went to Catholic school knew the word "bastard" and what it meant. The kids at my public school didn't care. What was that girl's name? Theresa Carlotti. She made my life hell. Her perfect little nose and her perfect little butt had "cheerleader" written all over it by the age of eight.

"Skyler's a bastard," she'd say to her future cheerleading squad, whenever I was in earshot. Sometimes "fat" was added as a qualifier. I didn't engage, hoping they'd get bored if they didn't see blood.

Anyway, back at the Bible meeting, Matthew went on for awhile, his voice breaking occasionally from the emotional strain. Somehow I didn't quite believe it. It was too forced. I started free-associating. Forced feeding, forced air heating, forceps, a display of force. I don't know, partly I don't want to pick on anyone's religious beliefs, I mean if you want to believe that some guy got strung up on a cross 2,000 years ago and now none of us have to suffer, well, that's your prerogative. Personally, I don't know what there is to be "saved" from, except our own guilt and my solution to that is just not to do things that make me feel guilty. But it's the brain-dead thing that bothers me, it's like all these people missed the Reformation or something. But maybe I just have a Protestant heart underneath it all. "Pagan," I can hear my Grandmother hiss, as she looked from me to my mom in fury. This because I said I didn't understand how the communion wafer could really be the actual body of Christ. I mean, how big could he have been? I was a kid and I wanted to know. But are there people—grown ups—who really believe it, or does everyone just kind of mentally skip over it? I mean, come on, it tastes like a wafer, right? You can see how well I did at catechism.

But suddenly everyone was saying, "Amen," so I mumbled along and then we all opened our eyes. I tried to look beatific, then remembered I was supposed to be male so the Virgin Mary expression was out. The only image of a man I could think of was J. Christ himself, twisting his mouth in agony and crossing his legs to cover his weenie as he hung there, larger than life above the altar at my childhood church. That wouldn't do either. I went for neutral. Maybe they'd think I was shy or something.

"Jen, would you like to lead us in a song?" Matthew asked.

Jen was short and chubby, with blue eyes and hands that stayed very still. What was she afraid of doing, I wondered while I watched her. She wasn't pretty and I was sure it bothered her.

"Sure," she smiled. She took a deep breath and opened her mouth and started singing—I kid you not—*Michael Row Your Boat Ashore*. What was next, *Onward Christian Soldiers*?

Everyone joined in, swaying while they sang. I kinda muttered while I moved my lips. I figured they should hear my voice as little as possible and anyway I didn't know the words after the obvious first verse. All I had to really deal with were a few hallelujahs.

What was harder to deal with were the looks I was

getting from some of the women. I guess I did make a cute boy. They were trying to look innocent and inviting at the same time, sexy in a God-fearing way or something. Utterly submissive was how it came out, but I've seen that look before, on women who wouldn't be caught dead at a Christian meeting. It usually happens on the subway, especially in cold weather when I have my big jacket on, and they think I'm a boy. I probably look sweeter than most. Let's face it, I didn't grow up with a penis and the inalienable right to stick it wherever I wanted. So the women smile and I can't stand the awful, empty submission in their eyes. Would you please act like a human being with a reasonable excuse for existing? I want to demand. Instead of a combination sexy doormat/black hole? For the sake of womankind, would you knock it off? Okay, it's true, I want to shake them. Get some pride! And these Christian women were no exception. I avoided eye contact. What if they cornered me, demanding dates that ended in kisses impassioned by chastity? What if they wanted to marry me? I was getting way ahead of myself. Calm down, Gabriel. It's just a meeting.

"Since we have newcomers, maybe we could all introduce ourselves," directed Matthew. "My name's Matthew. I'm a senior and I found the Lord three years ago."

"I'm Lila and I'm a chemistry major," said the woman sitting to his right. Lila was kinda Tammy Faye Baker around the eyes. I found myself hoping she wouldn't have reason to cry.

"John Shipely," said the late comer like he was introducing himself to his public. Button down shirt, nice shoes, clipped hair. It was like corporate America did it with Jesus and John Shipley was the result. Scary dog.

"My name's Mary Anne," said the next woman, a slight southern slowness to the vowels. "I'm a sophomore and I was saved when I was twelve." She sent me a smile like we shared a secret and I don't want to admit it but I felt it tug at me somewhere deep and private. For a second I imagined what it would be like. I would start by brushing her page-boy hair, touching her neck as if by accident. She would wonder. Eventually, her eyes would start to close. Would she wear perfume or would I be able to smell her skin? Would she call my name or would she whisper?

Stop it, Gabriel. Now.

Next came Karen who was a senior. She also had a smile just for me. I tried not to notice. Beside her sat my guy.

"I'm David." No last name. Damn. "I'm a senior. Pre-med." I had about three seconds to examine him closely. The crew cut, the mean little eyes and matching smile, the short, broad build. He was carrying a notebook that said M.I.T. Wow, what a clue.

And last we had Jen, whose talents as a singer had already been shared. She didn't bat her eyes at me. Hallelujah.

My turn. I swallowed and tried to think baritone.

"Hi, I'm Jonah. I'm just checking it all out." This earned me a few more take me, use me, smiles from the female members. Maybe I could suggest Self-Defense for Jesus workshops for Christian women. Or was God supposed to protect you from men? I looked at Matthew to indicate I was done.

"So this is a business meeting," Matthew announced. "I guess it's our last one since the semester's almost over. So far on the agenda," he flipped through an official-looking binder, "we have, let's see, reports from the Students For Life Committee, and the Newsletter Committee and the Outreach Committee."

Which would be more boring: an hour and a half of prayer by Christians or an hour and a half of committee reports by Christians? Didn't they all need to go home and study for finals or something?

So we had reports. Jen was obviously the secretary as she wrote everything down and asked people to repeat things, especially money. The Students For Life, headed up by Lila, had raised $54 at their table outside the library. I tried not to clench my jaw. The newsletter was in great shape financially, reported John, as they'd sold the back cover to an "abortion counseling service." I really,

really had to bite down hard. And Mary Anne from the Outreach Committee wanted everyone to know that there would be a Christian presence next month at—yes, you guessed it—that homosexual parade.

Oh, you mean Gay Pride? I wanted to say. Hey, I'll be there too! I'm so glad some of you folks are out! The impulse to pull at my hair was starting to overwhelm me.

This is hell, I realized. Was this my just rewards? Had God won after all? Every chance she got, Mary Anne tried to catch my eye. I'm not your type, I wanted to plead. I'm really, really not. I scratched my head and didn't yank anything out and tried not to fidget.

Things went on like that until about 8:15 PM. There'd been some minor scuffles over whether or when to have extra prayer sessions for finals, but that was all settled. I was phasing in and out of alertness and trying not to look at the clock too much, when I realized that dear little David was speaking.

"We pay to go to school here. We pay a lot. Why do we have to miss classes for somebody else's religion?"

"Jewish students have to take Christmas off," Matthew said, in a very measured, very neutral tone. I could feel the tension rising between them. I could also see Jen roll her eyes and put down her pen. Whatever they were fighting about wasn't worth recording.

"This is a Christian country," David replied. He folded his arms over his chest. "At least it was before—" and he said a word I'd never heard before. Zag? Sog? Zog? "—before sog took over."

"Jesus never said to hate," placated pro-life Lila, looking from Matthew to David. "We can pray that everyone is saved. Let prayer be your strength, Dave."

"So the Fellowship as a whole isn't going to back this?" he countered, leaning forward and looking at everyone one by one.

Matthew sighed. "All in favor," he intoned in a flat voice, "of a protest at the Jewish holidays next September say, 'Aye.'"

"Aye," said David and John.

"All against, say 'Nay.' Sorry, David, you lose," he

said, without missing a beat, since everyone else voted nay. "I think we're done for the evening," he pushed on, not giving David another chance. My kind of Christian? "Let's end with the Lord's Prayer."

He bent his head and everyone followed suit.

I found myself intoning the words like those McDonald's commercials from childhood that you'll never forget. It was about as meaningless until we got to "and deliver us from evil," which I felt in my stomach as I said it. I wondered what David meant when he said it.

He was up and ready to go before the last amen had left for heaven, a surly, superior smile set on his lips. I stood up quickly, ignoring Mary Anne's and Matthew's attempts to reel me in for possible conversion, and headed out behind him. John had already caught up with him, their voices almost hissing in the empty hall. There was no one else around.

"Hey, David," I called, about ten feet behind him.

His head was bent to John's, but he stopped and turned to face me.

"Yeah?" came his reply. Not exactly friendly.

I kept walking until I was next to them. "I was kind of interested in what you were saying back there."

"Oh, yeah?" His eyes gave me a quick up and down, then he tried smiling. He didn't seem to have any trouble with my presumed gender, but I felt obvious and awkward. I didn't want him to look at my face. Wasn't it apparent that I had female fat, a strain in my voice, that I didn't shave?

"Yeah, like what was that 'sog' thing you mentioned?" I asked.

"Zog. That's the Zionist Occupation Government. Don't think for a minute the government we have was elected by the people, for the people. The Jews are hell-bent on controlling the world. They've taken control of the United States and they're making damn sure the white race is destroyed."

"Zionist Occupation Government," I heard myself repeating to encourage him. Sure. I had a nut case on my hands. "I never heard of that before."

John snorted. "Of course you haven't. Who do you think controls the media in this country?"

Gee, let me guess. The Buddhists? No, no, I know, the Methodists?

"Well, even if you're right about that, I mean isn't it kind of racist?" How do you make small talk with fascists?

David laughed, pouring on the charm. "No, no," he said, patting my shoulder. It was hard not to flinch. He brought his little ugly face close to mine. He had a short, round nose, brown eyes, a mouth that was way too mean to mean it when he smiled. "I'm a racialist. There's a difference. I'm proud of being white. I'm proud of what the white race has done."

Sure, me too. Small pox blankets, the Middle Passage, Hiroshima, Agent Orange.

"Oh," I said and didn't sound convinced.

"Why don't I give you some material to read?" he said, flipping open a binder and pulling out manila envelope. "These are some pamphlets that I recommend for newcomers."

"Well, thanks," I tried not to stutter, taking the envelope.

"There's Christian Identity meetings at my house every Saturday. That's tomorrow. You're welcome to come."

I felt my stomach sink lower. No, no, no. I had done this. I wasn't going to do that. No way.

"Let me give you my phone number." He wrote it down on my envelope in frighteningly precise script.

"So if I want to come tomorrow . . ." I heard myself saying. No, no, and again, no.

"Here's the address," he offered, in architect handwriting from hell. A neat, clean, pure white hell. This couldn't be real. "12 noon," he had underlined beneath the address.

"It'd be great if you came. I think we'd have a lot in common," he said.

"Thanks, David. Maybe I'll see you then," I said, disengaging myself toward the door.

"See you tomorrow, Jonah," John added, before bending his head back to Dave.

I could hear the other Christians coming into the hall, but I didn't turn to look. I wanted out.

TWENTY-ONE

An hour later I was doing sixty-five on the Mass. Pike, headed west. Jaye had lent me her car and all I could think about was one thing: getting to Judith. Outside, the darkness was hazy with streetlights and the only sound was the cars, chunks of steel compelled to impossible speeds. It was too dark to see people, those stray slices of someone you get as they rush past you and the only thing that stops you from colliding is a foot or two of empty air. The road was long and lonely.

I'd looked through David's pamphlets on the subway back to J. P. Apparently, Satan planted a seed in Eve's womb right next to Adam's. Cain killed Abel, his descendants killed Jesus, and all white Christians are now slated for extinction. The Jews are descended from Satan. The Jews control all the money and the banks. The Jews instigated both World Wars and the Russian Revolution, resulting in the deaths of 80 million white Christians. The Jews owned the German war factories of 1914 and 1939. The Jews have made it impossible for whites to afford children by instituting the federal income tax. The Jews promote homosexuality and abortion to destroy the white race. The Jews have forced integration on America so that the pure, white seed of Adam will be mongrelized by breeding with sub-humans. Especially Negroes.

Science has established commonalties between "The Negro" and the ape, I read as my train crossed the Charles. Beneath me, the water was gilded with city lights. Across the aisle, two children couldn't sit still and their mom was too tired to care. I pulled further into my corner, tucking a protective arm between the pamphlet and the kids, like a parent at a sudden stop, throwing an arm between child and windshield. It doesn't do any good, I've heard. But instinct is instinct, and love is love, and I kept looking around at Park Street Station while I waited for my transfer. Negroes have small brains and an animal smell, declared the pamphlet. They have long arms and weak lower limbs. I watched a little boy falling asleep in his mother's arms, all trust and need, his skin almost brown, hers almost white, and I looked at my own. Was anyone actually white? I couldn't stop looking for color, for what was the same.

Did David burn crosses? Paint twisted symbols on synagogues? Was he learning to build bombs or compiling lists of names? Had he killed or did he still dream of the day when a human heart would stop at his command? Power's fun, isn't it, Dave?

I was going eighty and I didn't care. I had to get to Judith.

The kitchen light was on and I could still smell dinner, something warm and sweet. It was a big room with tall windows and I wanted suddenly to see the morning sun come through them, to sit at the long farm table and eat hot cereal and listen to the quiet of earth and sky. I wanted to start again, before this week began, before my mother, before Diane's murder, before my job ran out, before everything started to hurt but I didn't know when that was and I was so tired. I could keep pretending but it kept on hurting and meanwhile other women lay on the cold ground waiting for it to be over, and other children ran through the autumn evening dreading home and wanting to go there, and other people stood in line refusing to be sad while they waited for money and all over the planet there were rooms of torture and bodies stacked higher and higher and through it all, David was handing out pamphlets. And he believed in them.

No one answered my quiet calls. It must have been close to midnight. I went up the stairs, the soft creaking of wood the only sound. Her room was at the end of the hall. She had dormer windows facing west and a bed covered in green that I had sat on but never laid on. It would smell like her and that was what I wanted. Just the dark quiet of night and the smell of Judith. I knocked softly on her door, and I heard her stir.

"Who's there?"

"It's me, Skyler," I was almost pleading.

"Skyler?" I heard her cross to the door, and then

she opened it, her eyes too big for the light, her dark hair wild with sleep.

"Skyler? Are you okay?"

I shook my head and she put her arms around me. There was such a terrible longing in my throat. I thought I would cry, but I didn't. I kissed her instead.

And then I had the dark quiet of night, broken only by her small sounds, and the smell of her, lingering til dawn.

I went before the sun was up, leaving a note to show I'd been there, leaving my heart. I love you, was all it said.

TWENTY-TWO

"So what I want to know is, is Gunther in on all this sick shit, or what?" asked Amy from the back seat.

It was 10 AM, I was driving, and we were on our way to Boston General.

"Yeah," said Jaye, sitting beside me. Her voice was hard and small. She didn't look up from David's pamphlets.

"These people really believe," and here she faltered, like the words she needed were too far out of reach, "that Jewish children are born with horns on their heads and they have them removed like goats or something."

We were all quiet for a minute while the idea settled in our stomach like rotten food. Eventually you vomit, before it gets to your blood. Was there a reflex like that for the soul? Instinctive and physical so you don't absorb what would kill you?

Jaye snapped the booklet shut and looked straight out the window.

"These people," she said slowly, calmly, "are out of their ever-loving minds."

She handed the pile to Amy.

"So," she continued conversationally, "you didn't want to go to their meeting today?"

I shook my head and realized that I was afraid, withthat cold, cold fear that haunts your heart like a ghost. I didn't want to go because I was afraid. It had stopped being a game or some wild, fun time, Skyler's Big Adventure. It was serious. Someone had murdered Diane. There were drugs, a crooked lawyer, an evil doctor, a Christian hate group, and a missing child, and I was afraid. If they'd killed before, they'd kill again.

"No," was all I could say, ashamed of my cowardice. I glanced at Amy in the rearview mirror. Her cowboy-hatted head was bent in study.

"You want to go?" I asked, trying to be flip and failing.

"Do you think I'd pass?" Jaye replied.

"Look, look!" Amy interrupted, bouncing on the

back seat. "Check it out!" she sang in a happy soprano, waving a flyer between me and Jaye.

"Amy, I'm trying to drive," I said. "What?"

"It's a flyer for some racist dickhead who's speaking today about how black people are genetically stupid."

"So?"

"So, if Davey put the flyer in here, Davey's probably going."

"So?" I repeated.

"So you don't have to go their repulsive meeting. He'll be gone this evening. You can break into his house instead. You seem to be good at it."

"Can anybody come with me?" I asked and felt stupid.

"Shit. Tonight's the Women's Caucus Dinner. No way," Jaye shook her head.

"I gotta work, too," Amy said apologetically.

I sighed and wished I hadn't asked.

"Well, I can try." I didn't like it but I had all day to avoid thinking about it.

I pulled the car into a parking space. Down the street loomed Boston General, two solid blocks of scalpels, bodily fluids and official-looking people. We had arrived.

It was crowded even on a Saturday. There was a kind of reception-information desk with three harried looking, big-haired women behind it, but they were as happy to ignore us as we were to be cruise right by.

"Head for the elevator," I'd instructed out on the street. "There's probably a directory near it."

The directory was one of those stand-up You-Are-Here deals, showing each floor in a different color like a shopping mall. Free sling with each broken arm! Kidneys: Buy One, Second Half-Price! Spring Special—25% Off All Blood Work!

Get a grip, Gabriel.

The Reproductive Health Center was on the West Wing of the fourth floor. We stepped into a waiting elevator without a word. More people followed. I was elbow to elbow with a man carrying flowers in one arm and a small girl in the other. He looked tired, his eyes grieving or getting ready to. The kid was holding on tight. On my other side was a woman in surgical greens with a paper mask hanging round her neck. She was tired too, but more exhausted than weary. She shut her eyes and I swear she slept. Nobody spoke.

We weren't the only ones to get off on the fourth floor, which was nice. Less conspicuous or something. There was a nurse's station directly across from the elevator, but like the women downstairs, they were happy to ignore us. We headed west.

The hallway was wide and clean and smelled like industrial disinfectant. Doors opened up on either side and I caught stray glimpses of IV tubes and people propped up on pillows and the blue glare of televisions. At the end of the corridor I could see a set of stairs. A young woman in a robe and fuzzy slippers sat in the hall in a wheelchair, recuperating nicely, or so it seemed. Nurse and doctor types strode by with purpose, while down by the end of the corridor a middle-aged woman with a cleaning cart walked like it hurt. Bunions, arthritis, varicose veins. I guess the setting out me in a medical frame of mind. We turned right, passed the stairs, and found it.

There wasn't a corridor anymore, but a wall with a glass door, and it was locked. The Reproductive Health Center, it said in plain black letters. No lights were on and there wasn't any other way in.

"Well, now what?" muttered Jaye, while I sighed despondently. I tried the door again. Amy did, too. It was still locked.

"Yeah, now what? Talk about dead ends," I said.

"You give up so easy sometimes," Amy chastised. She gave a quick look around. "Here, go wait in the stairwell," she said with a languorous wave of her hand. "Just wait."

"What are you going to do?" I asked.

"I'm gonna find someone with a key," she said like it was totally obvious to anyone with a brain cell or two.

We meekly did as told. It was a little dark and too

warm and the smell of ammonia was almost painful. Somewhere way above us a door banged open and someone trotted down a flight or two. We both jumped, and then sighed nervously. The echo was long and loud, making each noise indistinct, no beginnings or ends, disorienting, a vertigo of sound. I wanted to stand closer to Jaye, lean up against her or put my arm around her, but couldn't. I realized how little we touched and it made me lonely. The last echo wore itself out into silence. Then it was just our breathing.

About a minute later I heard Amy's voice out in the hall.

"Son of a bitch," she said and it sounded like she was crying.

"I hear ya," came the reply.

"He said he'd be at the office all day. How stupid does he think I am? I knew he was seeing someone, I knew it," Amy was playing it for all it was worth. There were probably real tears on her face.

The other voice was making sympathetic noises. I couldn't make out the words, but I did hear the unmistakable sound of a door being opened. A little more talking, Amy's quick laugh, then nothing. We waited another minute, until our door opened and Amy poked her head in to the stairs.

"Come on!" she whispered. "We're in!"

"How'd you do that?" I whispered as we sprinted across the empty hall into the cover of the dark office.

"Comes naturally," she shrugged, shutting the door behind us. "It was the cleaning woman. I knew she'd have the keys. I convinced her I was somebody's two-timed wife, and I'm looking for evidence."

There was burgundy carpet in the reception area, and soft chairs and little tables with shiny magazines about houses and children. The air smelled faintly like rubbing alcohol.

"Let's not linger," Jaye directed. "I'm going to try to access personnel files on the computer, see what I can find about the good doctor. Why don't you look for paper evidence?"

"I got patient files," I whispered back. I knew what I was looking for and I found it easily enough. The first room to the right was wall to wall file cabinets. The carpet was gone, replaced by gray and white tile. Everything was neat and precise. The black steel drawers gleamed. I remembered how Diane's obituary had directed donations to the Reproductive Health Center. Here. I wondered whose idea that had been. And I thought about my nightmare, the broiled turkey surrounded by carving knives and turkey basters. I pulled open the drawer.

Frasier, Diane. A nice, fat folder. Her treatments, which sounded horrible, had resulted in a live birth by C-section. Chloe Emma Frasier, six pounds, eight ounces. Her doctor, of course, was William Gunther.

I thought about the photograph, face down in Nathan Strauss' desk. And I thought about April Gordon's phone number in Joan's handwriting, stuck inside Diane's address book.

So I had two more questions, and the answers were just as easy. Gordon, April and Strauss, Joan. Both women had seen Dr. Gunther for fertility treatments and both of them should have four year old girls. Except Alexandra Leigh Gordon had died. As for Monica Ruth Strauss, I didn't know yet. But I was going to find out.

I put the files away, letting the heavy drawers roll shut on their own weight. What happened here, in these sterile rooms, needles and knives between women's legs? I didn't like it, not one bit.

Jaye was in the doorway.

"I couldn't get in. I didn't have the password."

"We should get out of here," I whispered back. My heart was getting loud from fear, which was definitely catching up with me. My skin was sticky and I didn't like the way my knees felt.

We went back to the reception area where Amy was half-heartedly picking at papers.

"No luck," she shrugged. "And everything down here," she indicated with her head, "is locked behind a steel door. Authorized personnel only. Guess that's where they do the important stuff."

"Let's go," I urged, feeling testy from fear.

We filed out quickly, Amy taking the lead. I shut the door and immediately felt better. Amy turned back into the main corridor and we followed at a small distance. I saw her whisper something to the cleaning woman, who I guessed would lock up behind us. Amy waited for us by the elevator and we all got in silently. It wasn't until we were safely back in the car that I told them what I'd found. Jaye drove and I dozed in the back seat. Nobody said much on the way home.

TWENTY-THREE

I slept until three o'clock and by then Jaye was gone. There was a message on the machine from Sarah from *The Women's Page*. Her care and concern was the gist of it, but it made my head hurt just listening to it.

"If you need my car," said a note on the table, weighed down by Jaye's keys. I took her up on it.

I washed my sleepy head, resurrected the ace bandage and left the house in Jonah persona. I didn't have a plan, only the same cold dread in my stomach. I just want it all to be over, I begged as I turned on the car radio and then I wondered if I was praying. I turned the volume louder to drown out the thought.

David lived on a narrow street half way between Central and Harvard squares. The house was a small Victorian, painted a soft, creamy peach, which I hadn't expected. I'd imagined something hard and ugly, gray stone with lots of cement and beer cans instead of a garden, broken windows or other things that hurt and hinted at violence. But the street was quiet and calm and the house seemed cared about. I boy-walked up the porch stairs and read over the mail boxes. D. Peterson lived on the second floor, with one P. Manning. The street was so quiet for the middle of the city. Everything sounded far away. The door to the front hall was unlocked. I stepped inside.

It was quieter still, the smell like old wood. There were two apartments on the first floor, each with a steel door and a peephole, a twentieth century contrast to the wide, wooden staircase that led up. I could see where each riser had been worn down into a gentle curve. A single beam of sun shot through a small window. I watched the dust glimmer, motionless in the light. Balance is constant movement, someone had told me. Watching the dust I didn't believe it.

The stairs waited. I had to do it and I didn't want to. I put my hand on the banister as if stairs were an upper body activity and started up.

At least there was noise at the top of the stairs, and it was coming from David's apartment. "Second floor, left," he'd written on my envelope. It was the sound of a television. There were crowds roaring and a male narrator and then a real, live person making a kind of sloppy, excited vowel sound. We're talking intelligence. Somehow it fortified me. I knocked briskly on the door.

In a minute it was opened by a young white male of the species. He had on a Boston College t-shirt and a beer. I got the feeling both were permanent accessories, like tattoos or those "foundation garments" your grandmother wore. He didn't seem scary, just tall.

"Yeah?" he grunted.

I took a quick breath and dove in. "Hi, um, my name's Jonah and I was here at, you know, David's meeting today?"

I was gambling that Mr. Manning didn't attend or that the beer had blurred his memory or his judgment or both.

"Is David back yet?" I asked.

Boston College shook his head and grunted in the negative.

"Oh. Well, I left my appointment book here by accident. David said he'd leave it out for me."

His head had turned back to the tv like a compass needle seeking north. I decided it was time to be directive.

"Well, can I come in and get it?"

He shrugged and left the door for parts closer to the television. I decided he meant yes.

"Thanks," I said, like we were having a real conversation. He settled himself in a large green armchair, a bag of potato chips at his feet like a loyal pup. I don't even know if he heard me.

So it was that easy. I headed down the hardwood hall. There was a green-tiled bathroom, a kitchen with too many dirty dishes, and two bedrooms. I could tell which was David's right away. I guess the framed photograph of Hitler made it kind of apparent.

Other than that, his room seemed so normal. An

unpainted pine chest of drawers, a fairly neat closet, a desk weighted down with text books, an unmade bed with blue plaid sheets. I felt myself recoiling at the sight of his bed and realized I could smell him, the faint scent of a human body, and I didn't like it. Then I realized what I was seeing, half hidden by his pillow. A bra. A woman's bra and I knew whose it had been, I just knew. He probably shoved it in his pocket when no one was looking, last Sunday at Diane's house. I thought I was going to start screaming, but I didn't. I kinda lost it instead. I had to get out of there and I wanted to hurt someone, something visible, broken, pieces cracked and strewn, and through it all I still needed to know what was happening to Chloe Frasier. I yanked open my knapsack and started grabbing things, papers on the dresser, a stack of pamphlets off the desk, their covers were newsprint photos of concentration camp victims, no flesh, no hair, just eyes, reduced to the bare bones of human, and all across the page the word "Lies, Lies, Lies," was written. A notebook beside them. Another pile of papers, they looked like math assignments but I didn't care, and I grabbed Diane's bra and shoved it in on top. I was yanking at the zipper but it didn't want to close and I could feel a sound starting in my throat, some awful howling noise that wanted out. I shut my mouth tighter and I could feel it clawing at me, wild and trapped and I was going to go crazy if I didn't get the fuck out of there. I gave up on the zipper. I picked up my knapsack and tucked it tight under my arm and hoped nothing would fall out and didn't really care. I tried not to run back down the hall.

"Thanks," I said to P. Manning, who raised his hand toward me and didn't look. I held my knapsack tighter and shut the door behind me.

Down the stairs two at a time, I wanted out, my feet were making too much noise, but they also couldn't make enough, for all that anyone cared. Lies. Barbed wire of the soul. Lies, lies, lies. A dead woman's bra. Had he killed her? Six million dead. I was out the door, still running, still not making a sound, still wanting to scream. The houses were quiet. No one was home, no one ever fucking was.

I did scream eventually. I don't remember driving home, except somewhere on the Mass. Ave. Bridge, when I opened my mouth and let something out. I don't like to remember.

TWENTY-FOUR

I sat on the floor by my bed, contemplating my bowl. It was empty. There was more pasta on the stove and I wanted it but not because I was hungry. I pushed the bowl away. The sun was wrapping up another day and I didn't want her to leave. Like how I used to beg my mom not to go to work when I was four, I had felt so alone in an empty world. Now the sun was leaving me and it would be dark and cold. Jaye wouldn't be home for hours. I shivered and turned on both lights.

My knapsack lay in wait on the bed, filled with goodies from Dave's. I sat down beside it with a sigh. Was it too late to turn back? Make you a deal, I wanted to say, let's not and say we did. I won't tell if you won't tell. But there was no hope for it. I reached inside and pulled everything out.

I didn't want to see the picture again, but it wasn't as bad the second time around. Lies, Lies, Lies, was still printed across their faces, more dehumanizing somehow than tattooed numbers. I slowly put the pamphlets to one side, like my gentleness could restore something. I'd look through them later. One spiral notebook was filled with notes in that horribly neat handwriting. For a chemistry class or something. There were lots of capital letters paired with little ones, and numbers tagging along here and there. I'd also swiped a stack of homework assignments, all neatly stapled in the left corner and all with a red-penciled check mark on top. Dave did his homework. What a good boy. I flipped open another notebook. "Gunther" was the first word. "T 1—3" was written underneath it.

I blinked and read it again. Gunther. The realization began to dawn. He probably taught at M.I.T. That could be the connection, how Dave and him had met. Then "T 1—3" would be his office hours. But there was no building or room number. Damn, damn and more damn. I thumbed through the pages, looking for some random guidance or divine intervention, something to tell me what to do next. There was nothing except page after page of that perfect printing, aiming for the heart of each spoken sentence, trying to catch the essence of what had been said: *adjacent operator gene initiates protein synthesis.* Words are animate, I thought suddenly, moving through time and space on their own. The attempt to hold them still seemed useless, a waste, utterly beside the point. Maybe it was really an attempt to hold them accountable: hey words, I know you were here, you left a mark, a meaning, a change in the universe. Meanwhile they were long gone, quick as fish slipping down a dark river. We want something to last, but nothing does. The tragic flaw of the human race. I looked back to the notebook.

Adjacent operator gene, I read again and felt a nasty shiver in my spine. I didn't like it. Nazi Youth and genetics don't make a good match to my mind.

I jumped up and went for the phone. One call to information, one to the M.I.T. switchboard, and I had his office location. Luckily I'm not always so organized. I knew I hadn't thrown out my trusty M.I.T. map, so I poked around on my desk until I found it, patiently waiting under my sorry attempts at a resume. I circled the relevant building with a bright pink felt tip, stuck the map in my back pocket, and headed out the door. An address. All I wanted was the man's address.

I took Jaye's car again. The solidity of steel and the promise of a quick getaway were a little reassuring, and I was scared. Not directly about what I might find at M.I.T., but about all of it. I tried not to engage body, mind or soul, just the automatic pilot. Luckily, it knew how to drive.

I parked in a faculty lot near my destination, figuring on a Saturday night no one would care, or not enough to tow me. It was about seven and the sun was heading down, the sky all orange with farewells. I found the soundtrack to the Sound of Music running through my brain, that really corny scene where all the kids sing goodnight at the party. It made me embarrassed, like I'd been caught singing it out loud or something. Nobody can read your mind, I told myself, heading toward the building.

I could see lighted windows, so there were definitely people in there. Sure, the ones with nothing else to do on a Saturday night except play with test tubes. Oh, be charitable, Gabriel. It's the end of the semester and they have to finish. Music drifted by from somewhere, some kind of pounding nasty boy rock that must have been very loud at the source. The evening air was warm and sweet and I was still craving green after the long gray winter. I shut my eyes for a minute, shoving my hands into the pockets of my denim jacket. Fraying cuffs, a patched elbow, one missing button. I love my jacket. The only friends worth having are the ones who'll take a spill with you.

Okay, time for action. A few wide stairs, and I was opening the door. It wasn't locked, but directly ahead was a security guard. Do not pass go, do not collect $200. I was supposed to show a valid ID.

Luckily, inspiration struck, and I decided to ride it out instead of stopping to think about it, before I lost my nerve.

"Hi, listen," I said to the man in the booth, a young white guy who looked bored but harmless. I'd decided to be a boy, as it was easier than having to explain that I was actually a girl, so I'd pitched my voice lower.

"I must have left my wallet in the lab this afternoon, because I can't find it anywhere. And of course my ID's in it. Could I go look for it?" I shrugged sheepishly, smiled and shut up. Jaye always says that's the first rule of fundraising: make your pitch then shut your mouth. The first one who talks loses.

The guy sized me up. I smiled bigger, trying to send out wholesome, earnest vibes.

"What class is the lab for?" he asked, an oral litmus test. Luckily I knew I could pass.

"Well, I'm pre-med, so I have a bunch. Today I was finishing up for Dr. Gunther's embryology." Nervousness made me want to chatter on, but I closed my jaw and kept smiling, channeling the spirit of Jaye.

"Sure, go ahead," he said magnanimously. Good thing he was one of those people who likes to feel important, a need which couldn't be filled very often at his security post.

"Thank you so much," I said, fulfilling my end of the deal. I started down the hall.

The first floor was nothing but empty classrooms, the second was a combination platter of classrooms, labs and offices, and on the third floor I found him. Or his office, to be exact. Dr. William Gunther, announced the plastic strip stuck to the door. Beneath it, he'd posted his office hours and phone number. I tried the knob on the off chance that this was my lucky day. Needless to say, it wasn't. So now what. I considered for a minute. There wasn't anybody around. I tried the door again. It wasn't a tight fit, and I could see there wasn't a dead bolt. Maybe it was time to try a credit card. When I lived in the dorms my first year at college—a 100 percent miserable experience for a young lesbian feminist—everyone was forever locking themselves out of their rooms. Me and this guy Ranjit, who lived downstairs on the boy floor, got reputations as the resident experts. I don't know what his story was. Mine was all attitude. I'd gotten used to breaking into my own house as a kid, when I'd lost my key and my mom wasn't home yet, so this dorm stuff seemed like no big deal. Of course the dorm doors had been in a whole other class of cheap, but the doctor's door wasn't exactly high security, either. I opened my wallet and chose my weapon.

What I ended up using was my BPL card. It hurt, but realistically speaking it was the easiest one to replace. A driver's license could run me fifty bucks, a food stamp card replacement meant dealing with the Department of Public Welfare equivalent of Ms. Allen, and my credit card would be a pain in the butt. The library card would be quick, easy and a comparatively painless $5. I reminded myself of all of this repeatedly, while I spent ten minutes mangling it on Dr. Gunther's door. When the door finally clicked open, I think it was just trying to acknowledge my persistence, but then I have a tendency to anthropomorphise everyday objects. Makes the world a more interesting place, you know?

The room wasn't particularly big, but there were

built-in bookshelves on two walls and a large window behind a big wooden desk which faced the door. I didn't turn the light on as there was still just enough natural light to see by.

The main thing I wanted was simple. I wanted his address. Proof of drug dealing, murder, or other criminal activity would be a definite bonus, but if I could just get his address. He had Chloe, the housekeeper had told me as much, and if I could just find his address I would feel so much better about life.

I went to the desk, took a seat and started searching. Everything was neat, organized and professional and nowhere could I find a home address. The guy had to live somewhere. I was getting really frustrated plus I was getting more and more nervous. Every minute pushed my heart rate up a little more. What a way to get your aerobic exercise. His desk held what you'd expect: research papers from colleagues, a pile of students homework assignments, and official looking journals. I renamed them as I finished pawing through his drawers. *Embryology Today. Fetal Development and Fashion. Reproductive Lifestyle.* I couldn't understand most of it, only enough to see that I didn't need to. I gave up on the desk and looked around again. There were the bookshelves, a few chairs on the other side of the desk, and a little closet. I got up and went to the closet. There was a suit jacket and three empty hangers. Above those was a narrow shelf. I patted down its length, finding nothing but a small manila envelope. I took it over to the window for more light.

There wasn't anything written on it and it was sealed. I was considering whether or not to open it when I heard footsteps.

Down the hall.

Coming toward me.

I held my breath. The footsteps got closer and closer. I felt my knees start to give up while my heart started doing double back flips. The footsteps stopped outside the door. I dove under the desk, the only available hiding place, curling up in the hollow spot and pulling the chair in behind me. Meanwhile keys were jingling and the sound of the correct one being inserted made me sick to my stomach. I'm not cut out for a life of crime, I found myself silently reciting, I'm not, I'm not, I'm not.

The door opened and the light went on. I shut my eyes ostrich-like: if I can't see them, they can't see me. Then I tried to make my mind go blank, as if thoughts would disturb the ions, the air, drawing him to me. It occurred to me in a flash that there wasn't much to this room besides the desk: he'd be beside me in a second, pulling out his chair to sit down. *So long, farewell, auf viedersen, good bye* . . . the ditsy soundtrack to my demise.

But he didn't. Instead, I heard the sound of a door—the closet door—then some movement.

"Damn," he said, just under his breath. I suddenly realized that I was still holding the manila envelope. That it had been the only thing in the closet. That he was looking for it and I had it. *I'd like to stay and taste my first champagne* . . .

The closet door shut, the light went off, and just as quickly as he'd arrived he was gone. I listened to his footsteps retreating down the hall, my starved lungs wobbling like they were drunk. Air never tasted so good. I opened my eyes and breathed a few more times.

I had to get out of there. Would he be back? Would he call security? The realization that my fingerprints were all over the place sank in my stomach like day-old french fries. I really had to get out of there. I scrambled to my feet and tucked my loot inside my jacket.

I opened the door a crack and put an eye to it. Nothing. The hall was empty. Out I went, shutting the door behind me with a happy click. I found the nearest staircase and took the stairs as fast as I could. *Like a bat out of hell,* popped into my mind, except I liked bats and I didn't believe in hell, besides the one we've made here on earth. *Like a dyke out of Nebraska,* I tried.

Back on the first floor, I went as fast as my legs would take me without running. I was about to turn the corner into the entrance hall when I realized there were voices. I stopped cold, trying to hear.

"Maybe five-nine, kind of medium build. He had

short brown hair," said the security guard, his tone eager and apologetic.

"If he comes back this way, don't let him go. I have a feeling—" it was Dr. Gunther's voice and I didn't wait to hear the rest. I turned and started back the way I'd come. There had to be more than one exit. Meanwhile the hallway had gotten so long and my back felt so exposed. Any minute he could come back this way. I started running on tiptoe. *The sun has gone to bed and so must I . . .*

I turned a corner and felt marginally better. I kept up my tiptoed pace, passing empty classrooms with open doors. Ahead I saw a lighted red Exit sign and then I felt even better. I was trying not to breath too loud, trying to keep my terror-stricken vibes to myself. Emergency Exit Only After 9 PM. ALARM WILL SOUND! announced the door. It wasn't nine yet, but even if it had been I wouldn't have cared. I pushed it open.

Outside, the air was sweeter than anything I'd ever known. The twilight had grown softer and the sky seemed huge with purple. I was so happy to be alive, in one piece, free, as I fell into step behind a pair of laughing boys. They smelled like aftershave and I didn't care. I was on some kind of adrenaline high that made every detail sharp and luscious with life. I breathed and breathed and kept walking.

I found my parking lot, my car, and my keys, and then I was off, twenty mph, thirty, forty, surrounded by steel and speed, safe and sound. I unrolled the window and gave a victory hoot, and I didn't care when a typical Boston driver turned right from the left lane in front of me. Sure, go ahead, it's all wonderful.

By the time I was halfway home it had started to wear off. I turned off Centre Street into a Dunkin' Doughnuts parking lot, curiosity winning out over endorphin-induced ecstasy. I wanted to see what was in the all-important manila envelope. It was still in my jacket, nestled safely under my arm. The smell of deep-fried sugar drifted almost sleepily through the window, promising more than it would give. The act of eating those things never lived up to the way they smelled. Like Christmas when I was a kid. After all the build-up it was over in fifteen minutes, and all that was left was a pile of ripped up paper, some cheap plastic junk, and the realization that said plastic junk wasn't going to be half as fun as you'd been led to believe. I shut my eyes and breathed in some more doughnuts. Poor woman's cocaine? Or maybe it was just being a grown up: the smell was really all there was, so enjoy.

Okay, the envelope please. I ripped it open without further ado, and pulled out the truly dreadful. For the one millionth time I was left without words, with no possible way to put meaning to the actions of men. How. Why. And it's always, always the same. They were photographs. A little girl. Maybe eight years old. And surprise, surprise, she didn't have any clothes on. Do I have to say more? Here, her legs were spread, her own hand positioned over her stuff. Then a close-up shot. Then she was in a lace camisole, sucking her thumb. Then there was a grown-up man with a grown-up penis, and I wanted to kill someone. Tears wouldn't help, not her anyway. Neither would screaming or breaking things or losing my mind. I shoved the pictures back in the envelope. The world was back to flat and gray and ugly, all mean hard edges and empty pain. There was no life in the red and orange graffiti. The doughnut smell was sick. And I only had one thought left and it was alive and clawing its way through me.

Chloe. She was definitely in danger.

TWENTY-FIVE

I rang the doorbell a second time. I could see there were lights on. There had to be somebody home. There just had to be. The night was warm but I was so cold and I wished I'd worn more clothes. I shoved my hands in my pockets. It was all I could do not to ring the bell again.

"I'm coming," someone called impatiently. That someone was Joan Strauss.

The door opened and we stared at each other for a second.

"Leave us alone," she said and started to shut the door.

I shoved my foot in, and I won't say it didn't hurt, but at least the door stayed open.

"Chloe Frasier's in danger," I heard myself begging, "I have to find her."

Joan kept pushing, getting her shoulders behind it.

"I don't know what you're talking about," she insisted in a fury.

I didn't raise my voice, I just looked her straight in the eye and said, "What happened to Monica?"

It was almost like I'd hit her. Her face froze, all except the eyes, which turned tremendously sad, and she stopped trying to shut the door.

"Monica," she said, like she was admitting defeat. She was quiet for a second, sizing me up. Then she stepped back, letting me in. I crossed the threshold and shut the door behind me.

"Monica died," she said angrily. "What else do you want? I'm assuming your name's not Julie Cavanaugh."

"No, it's Skyler," I replied. "Skyler Gabriel."

She turned and walked toward the living room. I figured that was as much of an invite as I was going to get so I followed. Upstairs, I could hear Lisa laughing, those high-pitched happy shrieks that mean all's right with the world. There was a man's voice too, the cadence gentle and playful. I didn't want to go on with this. I wanted to be upstairs, where everything was okay.

Joan settled herself on the couch, spreading out

both arms.

"So what do you want?" she demanded.

"I want to know what's going on. Diane Frasier was murdered. I think by Dr. William Gunther. He treated her at The Reproductive Health Center and Chloe was the result. He was your doctor, too, and April Gordon's. Except Alexandra Gordon died and so did Monica. I think Gunther has Chloe but I don't know where. I do know Diane was here the night she was murdered, then she went to the bank and tried to empty her account, and she also dyed her hair. She was obviously leaving town, probably because Gunther was threatening her. I also know that your husband had a file on Diane, which he shredded after she was murdered. And that you gave her April Gordon's phone number. There's drugs here somewhere, too, but I think it was a set-up by the doctor. He lives in Wellesley, and the prescription pills in Diane's bag had his name on the label from a drug store in Wellesley.

"That's all I know, except that they're not nice people, Joan. They're really, really not nice people."

That was it, the end of the line, everybody off. I shut my mouth and waited.

"You're good," Joan granted with a nod. "God, I wish I had a cigarette. Do you smoke? Neither do I, anymore."

"All right, you want the whole story?" Her voice was slow and pitched soft but the effect was more intense. I could feel a shiver start somewhere in my stomach. "You're right, Gunther was my doctor. We were having trouble conceiving and I really wanted a baby. So we live in Boston, the medical capital of the world. Gunther was supposed to be the best. Well, he got us a baby, so I guess he was good. And yes, that's where I met Diane and April. In the waiting room. Diane and Jonathan had just bought that house and she took my phone number for landscape design. Diane wanted a home, not just a house, you know? She grew up in foster care. She'd also had an illegal abortion when she was a young girl, awful story," Joan said with a wave of her hand. She took a moment to continue.

"That's why she was having trouble conceiving. And Jonathan's family disowned him when he married her. Because she wasn't Jewish. Look, it's a real concern," she said, answering a question I hadn't asked. "I mean, Jews have won a level of acceptance in America that our great-grandparents couldn't have imagined. We don't have to live in segregated ghettoes. Intermarrying isn't prohibited by law. There aren't quotas anymore to keep us out of universities. But there's another side to it. You know the old joke," she insisted graciously. "What do you call the grandchildren of a Jew who marries a goy?"

I shook my head mutely.

"Christians. So it's a real concern, and I understand that. I wouldn't have sat shiva for him, but I understand."

"So neither of them have family and they're desperate for this baby. Gunther was able to give them a miracle, too. Or so it seemed."

"So. So I have all my treatments—and believe me, they are not pleasant—and I'm finally pregnant, and Gunther starts getting strange. At first, well, I'd say he was over-solicitous. He did everything short of forbidding me to work or have a drink. Things like that. He'd refer to 'my baby', meaning his? It was . . . it was a little unnerving. But I was so grateful, I was willing to make allowances. And it wasn't anything that overt. We had a big fight over whether I'd have a C-section. Why have surgery you don't need? I wanted to have a baby, not wake up and find one. I decided it was old-fashioned medical sexism, and he backed off, but I didn't like it."

She paused again, considering, mapping out a narrative she'd never told.

"It was after Monica was born that things got out of hand. The man called at least once a week to check up on 'his' little girl. The first month or two, we weren't really concerned. We didn't really notice, we were so busy with the new baby. But about the time we started to get bothered by his phone calls, we also began to realize that there was something wrong with Monica. So we went from running tests on me to running tests on her. And Dr. Gunther was there every step of the way. The medical system is so overwhelming, who's going to complain you've got a doctor in your corner? A good doctor, too. One of the best. He got us in to see specialists we would have had to wait weeks to see. So he calls on the phone a lot. I figured he was just overinvolved or something, I don't know.

"But Monica. There was something wrong with her. None of them ever figured out what. She was born with tumors—subcutaneous neurofibromas, were the words the specialist used. And I'm saying, Tumors? Are you telling me my baby has tumors?"

There was silence here, and I waited, wishing I had a cigarette to give her so we could both pretend that was why she had stopped talking.

"She was probably retarded or at least developmentally delayed. Also, there was already a bad scoliosis in her spine. She started having seizures at four months. Don't talk to me about terror until you've had a child with seizures. That's eventually what killed her. She died at eleven months."

She paused again and put a hand to her hair, which had been pinned up on her head but was half-falling down. The effect was somehow endearing, like she wasn't always the grown-up she intended to be.

"So we buried her and then we adopted. And I didn't think about Dr. Gunther anymore. Until last Saturday when Diane called. I remembered who she was. She said she had to talk to me right away. The woman was really upset. So I told her to come over."

"You're going to think this is crazy," she said with a short laugh, but there was no humor in it. She leaned forward.

"Gunther was every bit as 'solicitous' with her, but it had only gotten worse. He was calling all the time, and she thought he was following her. Diane said that he'd started insinuating that she was an unfit mother, especially after the drug bust, and that because Jonathan had died, Chloe might be better off in his care. Diane had been arrested for possessing drugs, but she swore she was innocent. She thought the doctor had set her up. She also . . ." here she sighed, one finger tapping twice on her knee, "she also thought that Gunther killed Jonathan. The police said he fell asleep at the wheel, but it wasn't late at night and there was no reason for him to be tired. Maybe the good doctor managed to put sleeping pills in his Diet Pepsi, who knows?

"It's not like she had any proof. What kind of proof could you have? A conversation here, a conversation there. There's nothing to go to the police with. There weren't any witnesses. But Diane was convinced he'd killed Jonathan and she was next. The man wanted Chloe, who knows why.

"If I hadn't had any experience of Dr. Gunther, I don't know what I would have thought. No, I would have thought she needed help. Anybody would. But I remembered how he acted, and so did Nathan. I'm not saying I believed her, but I didn't disbelieve her either. Until I saw the picture."

She looked at me, considering, a 100 percent not-funny smile on her face.

"You know how parents are. In the middle of all this she wants to show us a baby picture of Chloe, and I'm prepared to say she's an attractive child. But the picture."

She shook her head and leaned further toward me.

"She looked like Monica. I mean, they didn't just look a little bit alike. It was practically the same child, almost like identical twins or something. Nat and I just stared and stared. Just stared and stared. None of us knew what to think, but right then we started to get scared. We showed her our photo albums of Monica. I mean, Nat and I used to joke about how two people with dark hair for generations back had produced a blond child, but this. Nobody said it out loud. Nobody knew how. Did I give birth to some kind of Frankenstein? Was he cloning these children? Is that possible? Do we have the technology for that? What kind of God was he playing in his little test tubes? Was he rearranging their genes? I thought he'd given us a miracle, but was she a monster? She was just a baby, just a sweet baby who was too sick to live. What did he do to her?"

She wasn't telling a story anymore, because suddenly she was in it, and the end was nowhere in sight. We sat quietly for a minute while she gathered her composure, like wrapping a bandage over something raw.

"Then Diane told us what she'd found out about him. She'd hired one of those private investigators who specialize in checking out your fiancé. He'd been arrested for sexually abusing his daughter five years ago. Charged but not convicted. His first wife—her name was Erica—moved to Seattle, I'll bet to try to get away from him. In the meantime, Jenna died. She had something called neurofibromatosis. It's an inherited disease. The symptoms are similar to what Monica had."

She interrupted her own narrative, the present overwhelming the past again. "So, what? His sperm and my egg? And why? Maybe it wasn't even my egg, maybe she wasn't my daughter at all. I feel raped. On top of everything else. What the hell am I supposed to feel? And who the hell is going to believe this story?"

There was a bad pause. I sat without moving and thought about how much women need to wail. Just scream and howl until the universe or someone hears.

"After seeing the photo album, Diane decided to leave town. We all agreed she shouldn't tell us where she was going. We said we'd send her money when she got settled, anything she needed. And I remembered April Gordon. We'd kept in touch with a letter now and then, and her daughter died a few months after Monica. She never said what of, but I think we can guess. So I gave Diane her number in case she wanted to call her.

"And then there was the will. Because she didn't have any family, she wanted to make up a will that said under no circumstances was Gunther to be granted custody of Chloe. In case something happened to her. She was afraid he'd petition the court for custody. Frankly, he looks good on paper, since charged but not convicted doesn't count. Nathan drew up a will for her and everyone signed it. He kept a copy and so did she.

"So then she was murdered, and we have not slept since. And then you showed up, asking questions and breaking in left and right. Yes, Nat shredded her will. But what the hell are we supposed to do? Who's going to believe this? I don't even believe it myself. If it's true, then he's already killed two people. If we try to stop him, he'll come after us. We can't disappear. We'd have to create new identities and how would we support ourselves? I have Lisa now. Everything changes when you have a child," she was trying to convince herself by convincing me. "It could be true that Monica was just sick. Babies die. That's life. Jonathan was killed in a car accident, and Diane, well, she was distraught. She could have killed herself. What if she did have a drug problem? There's no evidence. It's too crazy, the other story." She was begging now and I wished I had a pardon to grant her. I would have done it.

"Do you know," I asked gently, "where Dr. Gunther lives?"

"Oh, yes," she replied wearily. "We had dinner over there more than once."

"Give me directions," I said, that cold, cold feeling in my stomach spreading like a leak.

"What are you going to do?"

"I'm going to get Chloe."

"You can't," she insisted.

"I have to," I replied and I was suddenly so tired. Upstairs, Lisa was probably tucked into bed. I wanted that kind of sleep and wondered if I'd ever know it again. Should I tell Joan, about the pornography? Ease the burden from my soul to hers? Would it help or was containment the best strategy and was she better off not knowing?

"I broke into his office at M.I.T. I found an envelope. Pictures. Homemade pornography. A girl about eight years old." I couldn't make myself speak in full sentences, the speech had to match the action, pieces, fragments, the broken thread of meaning, unable to hold against the weight of what had been done.

"You broke in?" she repeated slowly. "Then the pictures aren't admissible in a court of law. Illegally obtained evidence."

"And let's remember," I added, "he got off before."

I wanted to tell her what I knew, here on the fringe

of civilization. That nothing women said counted in a court of law. That the evidence of our bodies, the wreckage of a childhood, the daily battering of spirit and bone never mattered. I had more statistics than I could ever use, and still it was never enough to make women face this: there would be no justice. Not yet, anyway. Certainly not soon enough for Chloe Frasier.

"I have to go get Chloe. I don't want to be," and here I found myself begging, "a good German."

She gave a little snort and stood up.

"All right. Wait here."

She left the room and I shut my eyes. Part of me wanted to remember everything from this moment on, the deep crimson of the upholstery, the faint sweet scent of Joan, the sound of a man upstairs who couldn't carry a tune singing something slow and soft. And part of me knew it was too late.

In a minute she returned, with something tucked under her sweater. The teal green reminded me of Judith and it hurt, like I was lost somewhere and knew I'd never find my way home.

"Here," she said, drawing out a gun. It was big and black and looked so out of place in her small, soft hand. "This is not registered and you did not get it from me, do you understand? This is your safety, off, on. Just point it and pull the trigger. Don't bother to aim. Anything that gets in the way is gone. You have eight rounds in here. It's loaded."

She held it out by the barrel and placed it in my palm. "Take it."

It was heavy. I curled my fingers around it, trying it on for size. Holy Mother, help me, were the only words I had left.

Joan gave me directions. It wouldn't be hard to find. I stuck the gun in the back waistband of my jeans.

"I want you to know," Joan said at the door, "that I appreciate what you're doing." Her eyes said a lot more.

"Thanks," I replied.

TWENTY-SIX

The street was long and dark, attempting to be a country lane in the middle of the suburbs. The houses were set way back and the few I could see were huge. I found the high stone wall that marked Gunther's property and tried to look through the gate as I drove by. Two red dots of light indicated the security cameras that Joan had warned me about.

What did I know about child pornography and the men who made it? It's the only kind of pornography that's illegal in itself. Pictures and films of anything else—up to and including murder—are A-okay with the First Amendment. I've tried to explain this to countless women and they never want to believe me: it doesn't matter if he's found guilty of kidnapping, rape, torture and murder. The pictures are his to sell as he likes. And sell them they do. The free market meets male sexual sadism. Welcome to the world where our oppression is their speech. A growth industry, no less. Business is booming. What do you expect from a governement set up by slave owners.

But child pornography, because it's illegal, is often traded instead of sold. Maybe Gunther was going to swap his pictures for somebody else's, which is probably why he had the envelope in his office. He probably got tired of the same thing all the time, poor guy. Somebody else's daughter could put the zing back in. He didn't strike me as the type who needed the money, though the act of illicitly selling could have been a sexual thrill for him, too.

I made a right and then another, coming down the next street parallel to his. I was trying to estimate how far down his house would be. I was going to have to cut across someone else's property and hopefully come to Gunther's from the back, thus avoiding any unnecessary run-ins with the surveillance equipment.

I parked the car halfway between two houses. I got out and started walking quickly down the street. There weren't any sidewalks and the asphalt was hard and loud beneath me. On my right, an area of trees and brush gave way to a smooth expanse of grass and then, up ahead, a driveway and house. The night had turned cloudy and smelled like rain. There was no turning back. I stepped onto the lawn and started running.

The trees had all leafed out and I stayed beside them. The moon was wrapped tight in clouds, the light from the street didn't reach, and it was just me and the night. Hold me close, I begged like I had never asked a lover. Don't let anyone come between us.

I'm not a runner, by nature or design. I like my shoulders, the solid width of ribs and hips, the protection of size and uncertain gender. But right then I wanted an athlete's build, that slender edge that cut through space, I wanted those winter mornings when the air was sharp as a knife and the darkness lingered, just me and my lungs and the empty streets. I wanted the readiness of practice but all I had was fear and the hard metal of a gun, pressed up against my spine. I passed the house, about 200 yards to my left. My breathing was loud and sloppy and I hated the sound of it. I tripped on a branch, losing my balance too easily without light, but I didn't fall. The lawn ended in trees and brush. I was gambling that what lay on the other side was Gunther.

It was a suburban woodlot, not a primeval forest, and though I didn't find a path I didn't really need one. I didn't run, but walked, catching my breath as I zigzagged from tree to tree. My sense of direction had been formed on city streets and it needed cement and the tall shadows of buildings and the strange kinks of old streets. If I started to get lost would I know it? I tried to find the moon, but there was nothing. Something darted out in front of me and I jumped, an involuntary noise rattling in my throat. What lived in the woods at night? Only small things were left, but everything seemed huge in the dark. Maybe one day we'd wake to find ourselves swallowed by the forest's return.

Up ahead there was light and I steered toward it. I could see a house now, separated from the woods by a naked stretch of grass. I paused behind the last tree, preparing to run. It was definitely his house, the huge Victorian Joan had described, complete with white clapboard siding and a verandah. There was a swimming pool and a detached garage and small floodlights illuminating it all.

As for the house, there were two lights on. One was upstairs and from where I stood I could see it was in a hallway. The other was downstairs, but on the far side of the house. I could see a dim glow but nothing else.

I braced myself for the light, took a deep breath, and ran. The grass was soft as I pounded across it, faster than I'd ever moved before. The light was like a wound, wide open and too awake with sensation. I kept running and there was nowhere to hide and my blood was pounding louder than my feet. What would I do once I reached the house? Break a window, I thought wildly. Wrap my jacket around my hand and smash the glass. The violence would be a relief. But what if Chloe wasn't here?

The grass was behind me now, I was up against the house and still running, up the back stairs, a short flight I took in two steps. There was a small porch to keep off the rain and something with tiny green leaves growing up it. I grabbed the door knob and gave it a turn and it moved. The door was open.

Which should have been a warning, I mean why would somebody with surveillance cameras on his driveway leave his back door unlocked, but I wasn't thinking, I was moving, as fast as I could. I had to find Chloe and get out.

The dark inside was thick after the lit, open grass but I didn't have time to wait for my eyes to adjust. The house was completely quiet, the sound of my breathing an intrusion. I guessed it was around 9 PM. Where was everyone? There should have been people here in this huge, clean kitchen, or here, in the living room with French doors opening onto the verandah. But the only sign of life was the light, spilling over from across the hall. I went toward it. The lighted room turned out to be the dining room, with a chandelier and floor length drapes and a table that would easily seat twelve. Everything smelled like money, like wool carpets and old polished wood and daily cleaning. I had never been inside a house like this. Figures I had to break in. And still the only sound was my breathing.

I moved down the hall as quietly as I could. The next room was a sitting room or a drawing room or something out of a Jane Austen novel. In the dark I could see big floral patterns on the chairs and a clock was ticking on the mantel. Should I look through things? Try to find clues? When would they be home? Should I hide and see if Chloe was with them, then wait for sleep to make the world safe for kidnapping? I felt so sick.

The corner room was a greenhouse. There was a shallow pool with fat goldfish and the smell of damp earth and pots with plants from far, far away, tropical places thick and lush with green. Throughout the glass I could see there was no moon, no stars, only clouds. I wanted to rest here, my legs hurt from shaking, but there wouldn't be any rest until this was over. Not for me. I turned toward the last door. Shut but not locked. I pushed it open and stepped inside.

A short hallway opened up into a large room. A photography studio, it looked like. There was a long table and a sink and some hard modern chairs and lights set up before a white back drop and everything was cold, gleaming metal. There were cabinets on the walls and a few framed photos all in black and white.

I kept going. There was only one other room and it was a darkroom. There weren't any windows. I decided to risk a light and flipped the switch. The bulb glared down at me dispassionately. Everything seemed so flat after the darkness. There were trays of chemicals and a row of wooden cabinets filled with plastic jugs labeled Kodak. A clothesline was loaded down with drying prints. I looked closer. They were all of the same little girl. Chloe? Probably. She was blond and about the right age. And she had her clothes on, I saw with relief. Though some of them were getting weird. Somebody'd put lipstick on her and her too-big shirt was drooping off one shoulder. My friend David was in the next picture with her, winding a strand of her hair around his finger.

"Oh, God," I said out loud, closing my eyes. I leaned against one of the cabinets.

But it wasn't over yet. I had to keep going. I covered my face with both hands and tried to stop shaking. I had to go on.

I switched off the light and stepped back into the short hall. Enough. I knew enough. Upstairs. I had to look upstairs before I could decide what to do next.

I was halfway across the studio when the light switched on, and I was face to face with Dr. Gunther.

"Hello, Jonah," he said conversationally.

In a flash I could see my mistake. I should have given P. Manning a different name. But maybe David would have still guessed it was me. When he came home and found his stuff missing. He'd called the Doctor right away, of course. This was probably a severe breach of security. And the Doctor had gone to check on his little stash at the office. Finding it missing, he'd left the doors open, expecting me. In case I'd figured out his address.

"Looking for something?" he asked with a smile. He was just as big as I remembered and he was between me and the door. I made a mental note to myself: Sign up for Aikido ASAP.

"Or someone?"

Was it time to put all my cards on the table? Or was it time to pull out the gun? And then what? Kill him? Where was Chloe?

"You see, I think you're after Chloe Frasier, though I'm not sure why. I remember you," he added, eyes narrowing slowly. He snapped his fingers. "From the funeral. Of course. Poor Diane."

"Why do you want Chloe?" I asked. My voice sounded so strange. I wasn't shaking anymore, but I had never been so cold.

"I had an older brother," he explained patiently, while he drew something out his pocket. It was a small brown vial of liquid. "He was retarded and he was confined to a wheelchair. Pity is a disgusting emotion, isn't it? He drooled and he smelled like urine. The whole house did. I had to share a room with him. The noises he made were repulsive. I tried to teach him to be quiet but my father beat me. I was always afraid it would rub off on me.

That I could be contaminated by association.

"My second year in medical school I found out. I'm not just a carrier of bad genes. I have neurofibromatosis, too. That's the name. Degree of penetration is low in my case, so I don't drool or make guttural noises, but my brother and I are the same. And everybody thought I was the normal one. Smart. Clean. Neat."

He pulled up a sleeve of his white dress shirt, exposing half his forearm.

"Pigmented nevi," he said, looking down at himself dispassionately. I could see two small, brown spots on his skin.

"That's how it manifests in my case. But there's no doubt." He let the sleeve fall back into place.

"I read an account once of a woman who found out that she was part black. One of her parents was of mixed ancestry. She committed suicide. She said she felt contaminated from the inside out."

He put down the vial and looked at me.

"I knew I could clean myself. I knew I could father normal children."

Sure. And you'd also get to fuck somebody who couldn't fight back.

"Jenna was an accident. Erica refused an abortion. We could have had perfect children, if she'd just waited. My research was progressing. If she'd just waited."

"Research? You mean like Alexandra Gordon and Monica Strauss?"

"There are no mistakes in science, only steps on the path of progress," he replied, calmly, coolly, reasonably. "And I am making progress. My daughter, Chloe, may be normal."

"Funny. I was thinking of them as children, not mistakes," I said, watching as he took out something small, wrapped in white paper. Then he looked at me again.

"Did they catch on to what you were doing at Reproductive Health?" I asked. Time wasn't moving. It was because I was cold. That was it. I had frozen time, though moment by moment Dr. Gunther was still moving. I was afraid my teeth would start chattering.

"Not entirely. Though they did notice that all my children . . . looked alike," he laughed and it was not a happy sound. He ripped the wrapping off whatever it was he held.

There was a window behind me and there were chairs scattered about. If I broke the window could I get through it before he caught me? Should I take out the gun and demand Chloe's whereabouts? Then what? Lock him in the darkroom while me and Chloe made a run for it?

"What about David? Don't you know he's a neo-Nazi?" I demanded, like I could insist that we were having a normal conversation and therefore everything else was normal, too.

"We have an understanding," he replied.

Of course. Let me show you, young man. Keep it understated. Like mixing a martini. One part anti-semitism to one part racism, and don't hold back on the eugenics. Serves up nice with sexual sadism. I thought of David's finger curled around Chloe's hair. Had he helped himself to Jenna, too? Or had he come in too late on that one, so all he'd gotten were photos?

"How'd you get to be Chloe's guardian?"

"It was in Diane's will," he replied with that same slow smile.

Sure. You probably had one all drawn up and ready to go.

Or maybe not. Maybe he wasn't all prepared. If he'd been prepared, he'd have switched them when they murdered her. He'd had to kill her when he realized she was about to leave town. He must have followed her to the Strausses' and, knowing Nathan was a lawyer, worried about a will specifically barring him from guardianship. Then he'd had his will forged late that night or early the next morning. And then he'd returned with his little crew to switch them. Which is where I came in.

"Did you like my pictures?" he asked. So calm, so reasonable. "I don't hurt them. A lot of girls don't mind. Some of them like it. You'd be surprised."

I'm sure I would.

"Of course, they'll find the pictures in your personal

affects. And think they were yours."

What he was holding was a hypodermic needle. He stuck the tip into the vial and drew up the fluid.

"You see, Jonah," he said in that same, even tone, "you've made yourself a nuisance. And I don't know who you are," here he paused, looking from his needle to me, "but I don't think you're half the man you pretend to be. Please remember what I do for a living."

He held the needle and vial up to the light. "There. I didn't expect to find you in here. I thought you'd come upstairs right away. But this is probably better. No mess. It won't hurt," he said amiably.

He took a step toward me and I took a step back. This was how they'd killed Diane, I realized suddenly. The Physician's Desk Reference at the BPL. Prozac also came in a liquid. They must have injected her with a lethal dose, then scattered stray pills around and left a few bottles for the cops to find. Only I found them, too. David had helped him, I was sure, and probably that other guy, the tall, slow talker. A real gang bang. Male bonding at its finest.

"There's no point in shouting. There's no one home. I sent my wife out. Except your little friend Chloe. It's too late for her to be up and she has a big day tomorrow."

He took two more steps forward and I took two more backward and stumbled over a chair. He lunged toward me suddenly, with an almost sexual grace, and I got the chair between us, grabbing it by the back and shoving it up at him. He was strong but I didn't want to die. The chair hit him in the arm and he dropped the needle, which shattered into delicate, wet lace on the floor.

"You bitch," he said. Even in anger he just got colder.

I started running around the table. He was still between me and the door, but at least there was a table between me and him. Which felt like a slight measure of safety until I saw him pull something out of his jacket. It was small and black and mean. The moment stretched on and on. I was heading for the little hallway, one step, two, it was in slow motion, one thick, viscous mass of muscle trying to out distance time. I leapt around the corner just as I heard the shot and something faster than fast sang good-bye past my ear. I was on the other side of the hall, opposite the door. The only place left was the darkroom. I yanked it open and jumped in. I heard his steps, sharp and certain.

"All right, Jonah my girl, we'll do it this way," he said.

I didn't have time to think. Joan's gun was in my hand. I heard him walking, one, two, three, and then he was in the doorway but I was ready first.

I closed my eyes and pulled the trigger.

And again.

And again.

And again.

I wished I didn't have to open my eyes, but I did. I won't describe what it was like, but I also won't ever forget.

And I realized what I had to do. If I was going to get away with this I had to destroy any evidence that the doctor had been shot and that Chloe was alive.

I tried really hard not to look down as I sprang through the hall back to the studio. Time was going fast now and I was moving almost in a frenzy, opening every cabinet and grabbing at plastic containers of fluid, anything that said flammable. My hands were shaking too hard to undo the caps on the first few, so I smashed them instead, throwing them to the floor with all my might. I had thought earlier that violence would be a relief but it wasn't. The stench from some of the bottles was horrible and I found myself retching but I couldn't give in to vomiting. I couldn't, not yet. I stumbled toward the kitchen and had to turn on the light. There were matches in a drawer by the sink. This can't be real, I kept saying in my head as I ran back to the studio. My hands were shaking so bad I couldn't detach just one match. I ended up with a chunk of them and I lit it. They tumbled like a miniature Icarus out of my hand. Whose reward for what pride, I wondered as they hit the ground. Then I ran.

Through the house, back toward the living room,

and then up the curving staircase, two at a time, I was calling her name, "Chloe! Chloe!" I wanted to scream it but I couldn't. "Chloe?" I hit the light in the first room, obviously a guest room and it was empty. "Chloe?" Another bedroom, another light, still empty. My nostrils twitched involuntarily. A terrible smell was beginning to fill the air. Fire. Even the scent burned. Why the hell had I started the fire before I found the kid? What the hell had I been thinking? Suddenly a high-pitched, deafening noise came at me from all sides. The smoke alarm. Followed by the sound of a child crying in fear. Down the hall I ran, toward the sound. She was sitting in bed under a huge white quilt, holding a stuffed animal and screaming. She looked so small.

"Chloe, it's okay," I shouted over the noise. I don't know if she heard me. I grabbed her up into my arms and ran back down the stairs, through the wide, clean kitchen and out the door. I could see flames filling the studio and moving onward into the house. The shadows they cast across the grass were strange, bending and darting like living things. And the light was warm, all gold and orange. I held Chloe tighter and kept running. I couldn't stop until I reached the trees, I had to have darkness before I could rest. Chloe was still crying but I didn't have the air for comforting words. I had to get to darkness and we were almost there. There was a small explosion behind me and a surge of light and heat. I didn't look back, just kept running.

I reached the trees, lungs clutching at each breath. The dark was such a blessed relief. I set Chloe down for a minute, while I caught up on oxygen. She was still crying and I had to get her to stop. Any minute people would be here and she was making too much noise. I knelt in front of her.

"Chloe, it's okay, it's gonna be okay, but you have to stop crying. Chloe?"

It was no use. It was too scary and too late at night and she'd never seen me before in her life. She was still holding tight to her stuffed animal, a big green frog.

"Look, your frog's okay," I tried, taking one of its

legs and making it dance. No go. What was I supposed to do? I was gonna lose it myself in a minute. Murder, arson and kidnapping. Should I turn myself in? I was so tired. I shut my eyes.

I tried to make everything go still. Okay, Diane, I said in my heart. Diane, I've done everything I can do. She needs her mom. Please, Diane, wrap her up in your angel wings or something. Please make her stop crying. Diane, we need you.

I held onto the stillness, that quiet place somewhere at the bottom of everything, and Chloe held onto her frog. Her crying got softer. She looked at me with her huge child eyes and then she leaned toward me. I put my arms around her, remembering all of a sudden what it was like to be so little and have somebody big hold you. Her body shuddered and then she was quiet.

"It's gonna be okay, sweetie, I promise," I whispered into her hair. I looked down at the house. It was engulfed in flames. Burn, baby, burn.

Time to hit the road. I stood up, still holding Chloe, and took off running through the woods. There was still no moon but a faint orange glow from the fire lit the trees. Shadows wove across the ground and it was hard to tell what was real and what was only the absence of light. My lungs were rattling like some loose thing, a part that had broken off, and my heart felt huge and enraged at my demands. We were in darkness now, past where the light could reach, and I tripped on something hard, a root or a rock. I held tight to Chloe and twisted in the air, trying to take the fall on my side and not on her. My shoulder hit the ground first and pain ran through me like an aftershock. Chloe gave a startled little cry, but then she was quiet. There's always that second after you fall when you go, I'm okay, I'm okay, because you're still alive. I knew I had just royally fucked up my shoulder but I was still saying, I'm okay, yeah, I'm okay. I got to my feet and kept going. I swear Chloe gained about fifty pounds. The pain was extraordinary but I almost didn't feel it. It was less sensation, more an observation. And I kept running.

We reached where the woods ended behind the

back neighbor's house when I heard the sirens, wailing for all they were worth. It would be easier to run along the grass like how I'd come, sticking close to the trees that bordered the lawn, but I was afraid. There were lots of lights on in the house and any minute somebody could come out and look around to see what all the commotion was about. I stuck to the woods, foregoing the comfort of civilization in exchange for safety. We were parallel to the house when I realized it was raining. Big, soft drops of rain were falling all around us. Only a few had made it through the leaves to me, but they were gentle and cold. I could see people through the windows, a man in a brown plaid robe and a woman in something pink, staring out. They turned away before I had time to be afraid. My legs kept moving but I didn't know how.

Okay, I had two options: stick to the woods all the way to the car, or head for the road right away. I went for the road. Time was more crucial and I was running out of it. If the neighbors noticed the car. If a cop drove by. I had to get us out of there as fast as I could. I could see the road up ahead. A branch tore at my face. I needed both arms to hold Chloe and I had no protection. A sharp line of pain burned across my cheek. And then the trees ended and the street began, and I could really run. The asphalt was smooth and wide and there was nothing in the way except my lungs that were grabbing at air like a drowning thing, and my legs which ached beyond repair, and the weight of Chloe in my numb arms. Up ahead I could see Jaye's car.

Go, I commanded my legs, go.

I took off down the street. It felt more like lumbering than running, but bit by bit I gained speed and grace, and the street was quiet except for my feet and the soft rain. No one passed us. With one final push I made it to the car.

I yanked open the driver's side door and dove in, Chloe and all. I plunked her down in the passenger seat, shut the door and shoved the key in. The engine started up with no complaint. Let's hear it for Christmas presents from middle-class parents.

I started driving faster than I should have but it's hard to reign in instincts for survival, especially when they're pumped up with a mega-dose of adrenaline. Chloe curled up with her frog, so small in her seat, and I put my coat over her for warmth. We hit the Pike in about twenty minutes and I sang to her the whole rest of the way, though I think she fell asleep pretty soon after.

I only stopped once, on the bridge across the Connecticut River. I left the car running and stepped up to the railing. I threw the gun up and over and watched below for the splash, but it was raining too hard to see.

That's the only thing I remember, until I got there. I had to pick up Chloe and it hurt my shoulder so bad I cried out. There were lights on in the kitchen so somebody was still up and I wanted it to be Judith so bad. I held Chloe in my good arm and she laid her sleepy head against me.

The door was locked and I had to knock but I could see through the glass how Tanya and Star were sitting at the table, and Judith was there, too.

"Skyler," said Tanya in surprise, opening the door. "And who's this?"

I must have looked like hell. Their faces were all concern. I handed Chloe over to a pair of strong arms.

"Chloe," I said, as something gave way. "She's a genetic experiment."

Then I sat on the floor and cried.

TWENTY-SEVEN

I did a weird thing the next morning. It was Sunday and I went to church. Before anyone at Freerun was awake, I took Jaye's car and drove into Northampton looking for a Catholic church and an early service. I found both without any trouble. The service had already started, so I slid into the last pew, forgetting to genuflect. Oh, well. I never said I was cut out for religion. The air was heavy with incense and dark, since all the light came through stained glass. The ceiling must have been three stories high and for a moment I thought I saw birds, a sudden flicker of something that must be wings, but when I looked there was nothing. What you see is a state of mind.

I kept my coat on and watched for a little while, not kneeling like you're supposed to. Assume the position, please. This was a mistake, I decided, coming here. It hadn't even been five minutes and the priest was already droning. God, He, Him. There was a huge crucifix above the alter and it hurt. Why was He up there? Why did God make His own child be tortured? And why was I here? I certainly didn't want communion. Everybody was kneeling to pray and I couldn't join them, I just couldn't.

I slipped back out of the pew and was heading for the door when I saw an alcove. I went toward it, stepped in, and looked around. The walls and floor were hand cut gray stone, so the air was cool and damp. There was the same high ceiling but more windows, though they were all stained glass.

And there was a large statue of Mary, holding her infant child, encircled by candles. I gazed up into her face and then I wanted to pray. I lit a candle at her feet. The choir started singing out in the main room and from here, I could listen.

Holy Mary, I began in my head, Mother of God. Her smile was so gentle, and then I knew why I had come. Mary, I said in my heart, I killed someone. I didn't want to, but I had to.

That was all I could say. It was all there was. Just the truth, the whole awful truth of being a grown-up, of having to decide what was right, and then having to do it.

I stood for a long time, the silence in my heart almost a state of grace. I was listening, I realized, listening for an answer. Maybe the listening was an answer.

You'd have done it too, Mary, I said inside, for your baby. I know you would have.

I swear her smile got sweeter.

So that's what happened.

The Boston papers that Sunday all reported the fire.They said that Dr. Gunther was killed in it, and Chloe Frasier was presumed dead.They said the cause was suspicious, but involved chemicals from a home photography lab. I just keep reminding myself that 90 percent of all crimes are never solved.

I shouldn't have gone by myself. That's just the long and the short of it. I should have waited for Jaye and Amy and Katie. We could have thought of something. I know that now, but I guess hindsight's always 20/20. So I'm going to have to live with my actions. I'll tell you one thing, though. This lone individualist shit has got to go.

A very unanimous decision was made at Freerun to keep Chloe. Judith said she'd see what she could do about a birth certificate. She does work at a print shop, after all, and the kid will eventually want a driver's license.

I didn't tell them that I shot the doctor. I haven't told anyone. It seems safer that way, for Chloe and for me. I told them everything else, but I said that when I arrived, the house was already on fire, so I grabbed Chloe and ran.

Hallie, Tanya and Nora's daughter, is ecstatic to have a sister. She's decided they need a pony so she wants to do a "funraiser," as she calls it. I told her the band would perform *gratis*.

I don't know if Chloe's okay. Hopefully all they did to her was the pictures I saw. So far, so good on her health, too.

I flushed all the drugs from Diane's purse down the

toilet. I sent the rest of the stuff to Freerun—yeah, the money, too—'cause I think Chloe might want it someday. And I destroyed the pictures. I think about that other little girl a lot but I don't know what to do. I keep having nightmares that the house is burning again but I can't carry them both, only Chloe, and the other girl screams and screams and screams as I run holding Chloe. But I don't know what to do.

Nothing's changed with my mother. I'm sure she's still drinking.

I had to see somebody about my shoulder, so I decided on the cool dyke chiropractor in Jamaica Plain. Everyone goes to her and, like I told my mom, you get good medical benefits on unemployment. I had to put on one of those little gowns and my arm was one obvious purple mess.

"What the hell did you do to yourself?" she said in the nicest way. Okay, instant crush.

I'm taking a leave of absence from *The Women's Page*. Sarah says they're having a big meeting to discuss their policy about sado-masochism and pornography and she'll keep me updated. "Burnt-out" does not begin to describe how I feel.

The band sounds great and we're about ready for Minnesota. I think Amy's onto what really happened, or at least that something happened, but she doesn't push it.

As for Judith, well, it's still up in the air. I'm not really worried though. I have my good points and I know what they are. So I guess things don't always wrap up neat and tidy. But that's just life, you know?